Sa

Marble Isle

SALZWASSER
VERLAG

Sallie Bridges

Marble Isle

Reprint of the original, first published in 1864.

1st Edition 2022 | ISBN: 978-3-75259-434-8

Verlag (Publisher): Salzwasser Verlag GmbH, Zeilweg 44, 60439 Frankfurt, Deutschland
Vertretungsberechtigt (Authorized to represent): E. Roepke, Zeilweg 44, 60439 Frankfurt, Deutschland
Druck (Print): Books on Demand GmbH, In de Tarpen 42, 22848 Norderstedt, Deutschland

MARBLE ISLE

LEGENDS OF THE ROUND TABLE

OTHER POEMS.

By SALLIE BRIDGES.

PHILADELPHIA

1864

CONTENTS.

MISCELLANEOUS POEMS.

POEMS.

PAST, PRESENT, AND FUTURE.

Wildly dreaming sat I watching, watching the
bright sunset fade,
Saw its fairest colors mingling, till they met in eve's
dark shade,
And the twilight sadly veiling, veiling in the orb of
light,
Shutting from me all its glories, slowly leading in
the night;
Then the stars came, tiny twinklers, shining in their
distant home,
While the moon look'd cold and brilliant, hanging
in the azure dome.

Sounded near me then a rustling, rustling as of tru-
ant bird,
As there came a strain of music, softest that I e'er
have heard;

Then I turn'd, and there, beside me, was a strange
and gentle thing,
Seeming like a fairy spirit floating upon angel's
wing;
And its face was very beauteous, beauteous, but with
marks of woe,—
With some sorrow o'er it stealing, shadow of the
Long Ago.

First its soft dark eye was gazing, gazing deep into
my heart,
Stirring there the memories olden, of my former
life a part,
Calling up the buried treasures, treasures of the by-
gone years,
Till the dried-up fount was open'd by the gushing
of salt tears;
Then it beckon'd me to follow, follow in its airy
flight,
And I grasp'd its gleaming garment, robe of crimson
edged with white!

Onward, upward, then it bore me, bore me to the
scenes of yore,
Show'd me forms of dearly loved ones gone from
hence for evermore,
Brought before me brightest hours of my youth and
careless life,
Turned me from old dreams of pleasure to the
wrestlings strong of strife,

Pictured forth my early musings, musings of my future lot,
Stirr'd again past lonely yearnings, vanish'd thoughts long, long forgot.

Onward still it led me slowly, slowly through the perish'd years,
Mark'd my childhood's merry moments, girlhood's hopes and trembling fears,
Painted for my longing spirit scenes I grieved to know had gone,
Ever leading memory onward to the point whence we had flown;
Then it softly, gently faded, faded from my anxious sight,
Left me sighing, lonely pining for another vision-flight.

Then upon my sad ears sounding, sounding came a tuning gay,
Measure ringing, blithest, lightest ever chased dark gloom away;
And before me was a spirit, spirit of the Present bright,
With a countenance all joyous, shining as from inward light;
And its wings wore golden plumage, richer than the sunset dye,
With a smile of pleasure beaming, dancing in its sparkling eye.

So it quickly, tightly clasp'd me, clasp'd me with its
rose-hued hand,
Soaring over flowery pathways, through a restless,
merry band;
Show'd me friends I dearly cherish'd, cherish'd with
a heart-felt love,
Made me mid their many groupings with a silent
swiftness move,
Laid before me all the hopings, hopings earnest that
I knew,
Whisper'd that my fancy's visions, fair illusions, all
were true;

Then upon the rapid streamlet, streamlet of this
busy life,
Bore me on mid crested wavelet 'twixt its shores
with beauty rife,
Where upon the borders verdant Lotos-blossoms I
could see;
Told me that the moments passing ever joyous thus
would be,
Chasing off the faintest shadow, shadow floating o'er
my brow;
Murmuring still, with voice alluring, life would aye
be bright as now.

All the time its face was beaming, beaming with a
happy ray,
And upon the lips so gladsome changeless smiles
did ever play;

Then the hours flew by so swiftly, swiftly ere we
knew they were,
That we had no pause for sorrow, not a moment's
thought of care;
But suddenly its glory clouded, as it led me swiftly
home,
Then, with tones of wildest wailing, fled before the
great To Come!

Soon around me flow'd the music, music of a gush-
ing strain;
Fitful were its varied numbers, gleesome now, then
sad again;
While towards me, grandly moving on its wings of
sombre shade,
Came a figure that in nearing still a darker twilight
made;
And upon my spirit fearful stole a feeling kin to
awe,
As this image large and wondrous, strangely looming
thus I saw.

At its gesture, gath'ring evening faded with its shades
away,
Leaving there the heavens shining clear as at the
noon of day;
Soon upon the surface azure pass'd there oft a fleecy
cloud,
Then the gloomy storm rush'd o'er it with the
thunder dread and loud;

But these pass'd, and left it peaceful, peaceful and with calmness rife,
While the angel seem'd to utter, "Emblem of thy future life!"

Then it call'd before me faces, faces that were new and strange,
Others that were dear, familiar, but upon them all a change;
And amid the many groupings, groupings that before me fled,
Sought I many fondly loved ones; but the spirit whisper'd, "Dead!"
Closed I then my aching vision, that no longer I might see,
For it brought an anguish piercing, learning thus the yet To Be.

When my heavy eyelids raising, wishing more of fate to know,
Saw I but the figure moving, like a shadow waning slow;
And the night came like a mantle, wrapping in its mighty form,
While the wind and clouds were struggling like the coming of a storm;
But it pass'd, and left me sitting, sitting in the moon's cold beam,
Thinking of the mystic spirits, pond'ring o'er my waking dream.

Brought the Past its memories olden, olden scenes
of mirth and pain,
But had told me mid its teachings that 'twill ne'er
return again;
Brightly shone the happy Present, spirit ever light
and gay,
Still amid its fairest visions quickly fled its form
away;
Darkness shrouded round the Future, half its mysteries unreveal'd:
Now and Have Been both are open'd, only the To
Be is sealed!

1852.

WOMAN'S SIN.

"It is women who condemn the fallen of their own sex without pity; knowing little of their sufferings, comprehending not their struggles and wretchedness; only, like the Pharisee of old, they stand afar off, and thank God, in a loud voice, that they are not like to them!"

'Tis women have no charity,—
Oh, bitter, mournful truth!
'Tis they pursue the fallen ones
With never-ceasing ruth!

Why dost thou pass with scornful mien,
O woman of the world,
Yon smiling, wretched, outcast one
From Virtue's pathway hurl'd?

Is it because her form is deck'd
  In gaudy, soil'd array,
While on thine own the costly robes
  Such faultless taste display?
Does dress, then, so much difference make
  Thy haughty mind within?
Which dost thou hail with most contempt,
  The garment or the sin?

Or dost thou fear thy spotless name
  Might suffer, shouldst thou dare
With kindly gaze thy looks to send,
  Instead of chilling stare?
Dost dread lest man might coldly sneer,
  If thou shouldst gently speak
One loving word to that poor heart,
  The tempted and the weak?
Some might reproach thee for such act
  Whose sympathy is dead;
But He will mark the noble deed,
  Whose Son for sinners bled!

Remember how with earnest care
  A mother watch'd *thy* youth,
To cherish free from earthly taint
  Thy innocence and truth!
Perchance upon that once pure brow
  That bears the brand of shame,
No mother's lips have ever press'd
  A token of the name,

No mother's heart has ever yearn'd
  Above her child with prayer
That naught of evil's cankering weight
  The little one should bear!

Thou ne'er hast known Temptation's art,
  Nor all the woe that springs
From loneliness and bitter want,
  And poverty's sharp stings;
Life has not taught thee how to feel
  The miseries of the young,
When love and gold, with luring tones,
  Their siren songs have sung,
While hunger stands beside the hearth,
  A herald of the grave,
And not one warning voice to plead,
  No kindred hand to save!

Dost think that thou couldst thus have gone
  Through earth without a stain?
Couldst thou have borne its sneers and taunts,
  Its crosses and its pain?
Look well within, when thou wouldst scorn
  An erring sister's path;
Thou mayst have sins as dark as hers
  To meet the future wrath:
And think that all thy loving words,
  And every soften'd look,
Effaces some remember'd guilt
  From Heaven's record-book!

The angels weep when human souls
  From Virtue's pathway stray,
And joy in Paradise proclaims
  When sinning spirits pray!
Then what art thou, that thou shouldst dare,
  O worm of little worth,
To crush a heart that yet might soar
  Above its chains of earth?
Ere long the tomb will hide from man
  That thou hast ever been,
And death may make ye equals then,
  Thou and the Magdalene!

NOON.

At Summer noon the burning sunbeams pour
  In one unbroken flood of golden light,
By quenchless warmth the beauty to restore
  Of those fair blossoms hid by Winter's night.

The green-robed trees, deck'd in their fresh attire,
  Stand still and listless, wearied of the play
And murmur'd tales with which the breezes hire
  A leafy resting-place from heat of day.

The clock tolls forth its loud, sonorous peals,
  The sentinel that hails the morn's first rays
From towering steeple, trembling as it feels,
  In all its depth, the warning it conveys.

For this old clock is but the city's heart,
And each hour's knell the slowly beating throbs
That send its solemn pulse through every part,
To mark how much of life time gives or robs.

The weary workman greets the welcome hour,
And stops his toil to wipe his dusty face:
Glad of a respite from the sun's strong power,
He leaves his labor for some shady place,

Where, drawing from his basket's little store
The humble meal by careful hands prepared,
The sunburn'd brow grows brighter than before,
Rememb'ring "home," with loving spirits shared.

The cock, whose trumpet call had waked the day,
Has still'd the tones that swell'd his haughty throat,
And struts not now through regions of his sway,
While clucking hens applaud with flattering note

The bird is pining in his air-hung cage;
His tiny voice no longer trills the song
That tells of distant woods to travell'd age,
For whose cool shades his drooping feathers long.

The buzzing flies have ceased their circling flight,
Hushing their sleepy hum, and on the pane,
Like black-mail'd soldiers after lingering fight,
Sink, one by one, as on the battle's plain.

The eloquence of silence fills the air,
  Though life scarce seems alive in such still scene,
Save where yon humming-bird flits here and there,
  A living, sparkling jewel set in green;

And where the bounding heart of yon fair girl
  Flutters with each new dream 'gainst snowy vest,
Or where the balmy breath just stirs a curl,
  Passing through parted lips from heaving breast.

The rounded limbs in careless grace repose,
  The rosy mouth no impress bears of strife,
Where youth the glory of its sunlight throws,
  And Noon of Day keeps watch o'er Noon of Life.

The book has fallen from the nerveless hand;
  A dawning smile breaks o'er the blushing brow,
As, half awake, her hopes, a maiden band,
  The Future paint, unmindful of the Now.

And, nursing thus the children of the brain,
  The glowing visions that young spirits bear,
She roams an Eden free from sin and pain,
  And, trusting, thinks no serpent-trails are there.

May Heaven keep the glory of her way
  As pure and brilliant as her inward dreams!
May shades of night ne'er follow Joy's bright day,
  And Life prove all the Paradise it seems!

And evermore within the woman's mind,
  May Summer's golden beauty ripen love,
Till Death, the farmer of the skies, shall bind
  Its sheaf of fruits within the fields above!

1855.

ALPINE FLOWERS.

UPON the mountain's frozen height
  The Alpine Flowers bloom,
Like gems of purest light enclosed
  In some dark cavern's gloom;
And yet around their icy home
  They yield their fragrance sweet,
Although their modest loveliness
  No human eye may greet.

Amid the soft and fleecy clouds
  That float like angels' wings
Athwart the rosy-tinted brows
  Of Nature's snow-crown'd kings,
They grow, these fragile things of life,
  Mid parks and slopes of sleet,
Like signs from heaven dropp'd to mark
  The trace of spirit feet.

E'en as these lowly blossoms shed
  Calm beauty o'er the rock,
That echoes but the wild winds' voice
  And avalanche's shock,

As they survive 'neath mighty storms,
And mid eternal frost,
Where prouder plants soon fade and die,
Where lofty trees are lost;

So ever in the mortal mind
Some gentle memory lives,
That mid the height of worldly lore
An unknown perfume gives,
That nestles 'neath grief's bitter storms
And disappointment's power,
A fadeless garden for the soul
In sorrow's chilling hour.

When high ambition's aims have fail'd,
And earthly hopings die,
Like mountain-flowers sending up
Their incense to the sky,
Spring lofty thoughts within the heart,
Its lonely way to cheer,
Till holy deeds, like seraph-tracks,
Shall deck the prospect drear.

Remember, then, in wandering o'er
The world's hard, changing path,
We stand full oft on danger's steeps
And near the whirlwind's wrath.
Ah! cherish all the mossy spots
That memory's dew keeps green;
For know, when souls bear tender dreams,
That angels there have been.

THE STRANGER'S GRAVE.

THE fairies met in the church-yard old,
 When the moon was shining bright:
They sat on the blossom-spangled sod,
 In the shade of a tombstone white.
Their queen was throned on a snowy rose
 That bloom'd o'er a quiet grave,
While her court was group'd in humble flowers
 That amid the long grass wave.

They were tired of dancing on verdant lawn
 With carpet of velvet moss,
And weary of flinging the moon-ray motes
 With the chance of gain or loss;
They had drain'd their acorn-bowls of dew
 In their secret banquet-hall,—
A hollow stump on the green hill-side,
 Their table a toadstool tall.

And now they had come from revel and play
 In the dead men's home to rest,
And each silent, star-watch'd mound had rung
 With songs of a glad fay-guest;
But soon they had hush'd each elfin lay:—
 Their queen, Titania, spoke—
Her voice, like the warbling of far-off lark,
 The reverent silence broke.

Her robe was made of butterfly wings,
Of a glow-worm's gem her crown,
A humming-bird's plume her sceptre slight,
Her train of a moth's breast-down;
She stood on the tintless, satin edge
Of a pure unfolding leaf,
That emblem'd the stainless heart of youth
Ere life's page is marr'd by grief.

She told of a tomb in that calm place,
A sunken and barren mound,
Where only lay on the cold, dead face
The chill sods of dark, damp ground;
No flowerets shed their fragrant sighs
O'er that love-deserted spot,
A stranger's lonely and nameless grave,
Long by mortal souls forgot.

She bade them roam through the solemn aisles
And gather the ripen'd seeds,
To bring the sweets of forest and field,
The treasures of water'd meads,
And plant them over the dreamless head
That was lowly sleeping there:
Neglected by man, the stranger's grave
Henceforth should be fairies' care!

So, night after night, the tiny band
Bore from the green wood and vale
Their precious things, from the creeping vine
To the snow-drop pure and pale;

They wreathed an arch of the woodbine wild,
  And hung it with wind-tuned bells,
And wove festoons of sweet buds that bloom'd
  In hidden, untrodden dells.

And they stole the spotless lily-cups
  From the brook-shores where they grew,
Fit goblets to hold earth's sky-pledged wine,
  The sparkling and cloud-born dew;
The jessamine stars shed their silvery light,
  And clematis clusters hung
Like censers of perfume rarely wrought
  And by unseen spirits swung.

Thus toil'd each fay with unceasing skill,
  The midnight's mystical guest,
Twining a bower of magical grace
  O'er that dust-bound, pulseless breast:
Men wonder'd to see that desert mound
  In such sudden splendor bloom,
And lovers made it a storied spot:
  Forgot was its olden gloom!

And still, through the long, calm summer nights,
  When the moon, like blushing bride,
Spreads her veil of light, and fondly walks
  By her groom the earth's proud side,
The fairies rest on its flowery thrones,
  Where eve's trembling shadows wave:—
The brightest spot in that church-yard old
  Is the stranger's nameless grave!

THE MIRAGE.

ONCE, years ago, in Araby's far land,
A weary caravan had wander'd long,
And one by one, in desperate extreme,
Its way-worn stragglers had lain down and died;
While stronger frames still journey'd weakly on,
Though every sunburn'd brow but told despair;
For Thirst and Famine stalk'd on each slow step,
And Hope had almost ceased to lead the way.
Upon our blood-streak'd eyes the light stream'd down,
In one unquenchable, unshadow'd flood,
Till e'en its golden beauty seem'd a curse;
And some, whose brains unpitying rays had pierced,
Knelt on the burning sands, and pray'd aloud
For Darkness that should never know a morn,
For Death, for aught to free them from the beams
That drown'd their senses in such molten waves,—
And, kneeling, perish'd in a Simoon blast.

Behind, for miles of that scorch'd desert waste,
Were strewn the whitening bones of man and beast,
The landmarks showing Death's unsparing march.
Before was spread the same bright glittering scene
Of sparkling sand and blue unclouded sky.
North, south, east, west, that shining, arid field
Lay calm and still, and with the azure arch

Serenely smiled in mockery of our pain;
Till fearful oaths and imprecations loud
Burst from the quivering lips that raving swore
No Heaven could be beyond such lurid skies,
Since God nor Heaven shed no mercy down.

But suddenly all blasphemy was hush'd:
And some that erst had mutter'd cursing words
Now offer'd praises with repentant tone;
And men that had not wept since childhood's hour,
Cold, harden'd men, like very infants sobb'd,
As if their hearts would break with weight of joy·
And failing voices raised a feeble shout,
And tottering, faltering steps grew firm and swift,
As onward rush'd our worn and ghastly throng
With arms outstretch'd to grasp a precious prize;
For, lo! before our eager gaze were spread
The clear and placid waters of a lake,
With mossy banks enamell'd here and there
With groups of lovely flowers, whose Eastern hues
Seem'd like the remnant of some rainbow bright,
That dropp'd from its high home, and in the fall
Was broken, and its rich dyes scatter'd there;
The stately palm-trees bow'd their lofty heads,
The token-promise of abundant fruit;
And the calm waves where fell their lengthen'd shade
Cast up a dimpled smile of grateful love,
And wooed our panting haste with witching charms,
And like a herd of startled deer we flew,

On—on—with nimble footsteps wing'd by fear;
For Death, the hunter, caught each lingering form,
And love of life still nerved each drooping limb.
Still on we strove, nor heeded heat or toil!
On—on—the torrid earth beneath our feet
Sent up its hottest torture through our veins,
As if its central fire had upward cast
In one strong flame its genii-guarded might!
On—on—and on—no matter what our speed,
That dreadful sun still shower'd piercing beams,
That found their focus on our blister'd heads!
Yet onward—on—a fainting, wretched few,
We press'd with earnest zeal towards the goal
That still receded from our anxious view;
Till sighs of grief and groans of deep despair
Told where some life-chord broke, or footstep fail'd;
And they whose hope outsped their body's power,
Whose faithless step could bear them on no more,
Sank yelling, moaning, crawling, on the plain,
And there unburied rest where last they fell,
Without a grave where mourning friends might weep
Above the dust they had so loved in life!
While others, clinging with their bony hands
To hands as wasted, with a vice-like grasp,
Pray'd, with an eloquence from terror born,
Their fellow-sufferers for a little aid,
Urging each plea that human pain could use
For sympathy from lips as parch'd as theirs,
And promised stores of gold and priceless gems

To dying creatures but to heed their cry!
But want knows no compassion; and the men
Whose pity once would save a worm from harm,
With savage words, and murderous blows of hate,
Now dash'd their comrades from their side to die;
Forgetful of a time when they had shared
Each thought and feeling of old, happy hours,
And seeing not the disappointed glance
That told the bitterness and mute reproach,
That might have roused remorse or wrung a sigh!

But when the hopes of those who struggled on
Were at their wildest height, and the fair scene
Seem'd nearer, more alluring, than at first,
It quickly vanish'd from our yearning sight,
And left no trace of its deceptive green!
'Twas gone,—forever gone,—and with it Hope!
We gazed upon each others' face, to read
Some token that the dream was not dispell'd,—
Some cheering sign that Faith might yet believe;
But every brow was wither'd with the blight
Of this terrific, horrible despair!
Above was stretch'd that merciless blue sky,
Before, around, that hell of light and sand!
Naught else,—no water pure, no waving trees,
No blossoms peeping from the dewy grass;
That sweet Oasis was but false Mirage,
The Desert's treacherous, delusive scene;
And now 'twas gone—our destiny was there!
The wilderness our tomb,—the heavens our pall,—

Our only couch that awful bed of sand!
Stretching where'er we turn'd its glitterings keen,
It fill'd our cracking skin, and stung each wound;
It choked our throats, and coursed in every vein.
We would have slain a brother, in that hour,
Without compunction, and with barbarous glee
Have revell'd on the corpse, and drain'd each drop
Of boiling blood that gave our victim life,
Save that we had no strength to work our will.
And then—and then—we all went wholly mad!

'Twas strange, 'twas terrible, to see the change
That suffering wrought upon those wandering minds,
To list the plaintive tones and frantic sounds
Utter'd by swollen tongues and blacken'd lips;
To mark how Memory, strong in this dread hour,
Painted on each hot brain, with pencil true,
Her vivid pictures of each stage of life.
Some babbled of the bubbling brooks that spring
In shady forest-dells far, far away,
Beside whose murmuring windings they had roved
When hope was young and all the future bright;
Again they trod the gray and moisten'd stones
That broke the dimpling stream's calm, singing course,
Or aided, with the untaught grace of love,
Some trembling maiden o'er the rustic bridge,
Plucking the waving lilies from their stalks,
That, seated in some lonely glade, her hand
Might weave the woodland wild-rose into wreaths

Amid the snowy leaves of spray-born flowers,
While manly voice, in warm and tender strain,
Defied each lovely blossom e'er to match
The peerless beauty of her brow and blush!

Those, too, there were that told of fearful scenes
Of bloody conflict, and war's carnage dread,
And, gathering all of life in one last breath,
Sprang forward shouting some proud battle-cry,
Then, falling, died with that triumphant gasp!

And there was one that breathed an awful tale
Of secret sin and hidden, dreadful crime:
A high and honor'd man, his name of yore
Had been a country's rallying word of pride;
Men bow'd before him, and fair women sued
To win one flattering look from his cold eye;
He moved a star upon his shining path,
None deeming that the brilliant light of mind
But hid the darkness of a guilt-drown'd soul;
But now, as rang upon the lurid air
His shrieks of terror or remorseful groans,
The men who once had bent before his power
Drew from his hated touch each dying limb,
And feebly cursed the hope-deserted wretch.

And some pass'd silently, with breaking hearts,
Thinking of watchful forms that long would yearn
To greet the wanderer would return no more;
And all had ta'en a last farewell of life.

There was a fragile youth with golden hair,
That all the day had journey'd at my side.
Amid the trials of our desert march,
Without a murmur, with unfaltering trust,
His boyish step kept even pace with mine.
His slender fingers lay within my hand
Calmly as if no anguish stirr'd his veins;
Though ever and anon, as some new hope
To tumult roused the passions of my heart,
My throbbing pulse would leap against his own,
The cheering pressure of his gentle hand
Would check the raging burst of feeling's storm;
Whilst, pointing with the other wasted arm
Tow'rd th' horizon's verge, our cheating goal,
He spoke such words that even those who fled
With swiftest speed would turn to look again,
And wonder at the childish shape which breathed,
Like one inspired, such promises of grace;
With steadfast, shining eyes, that never bore
One trace of bitterness or shade of earth,
As if an angel exiled from its home,
And captive-bound within those walls of clay,
Was gazing from the windows of its cell,
Till it might soar from bars of human mould,
To meet, on shores of everlasting streams,
The seraph forms that hover round it now.
I do believe that mid that burning waste
One of God's spirits took me by the hand
And led me through its lava-floods of light,
Feeding my soul with manna from the skies;

For ever as he walk'd he chanted o'er
The lofty strains by Hebrew Psalmist sung,
Until the vision of that fairy isle
Perish'd amid those torrid waves of sand;
And then his voice grew quivering, faint and low,
Like the last sighs of an Eolian harp,
After some sweet and glorious melody,
Before the strings are shatter'd by the blast.
He wreathed his arm about my blister'd neck
And feebly bow'd my head till my dark hair
Mingled its untrain'd length with his bright locks,
Casting one glance of those large, wondrous eyes
In sad reproach upon my foaming lip;
And hand in hand, his breast against my own,
We sank together on the plain to die;
And all around was suffering, sand, and death,
And silence scarcely broken, save by groans
And dying prayers for some who ne'er would know
That those they loved were faithful to the last.

And thus we waited Death. The hot sun stood
In heaven's broad expanse, and downward shone
With smiling radiance at humbled man,
Like conquering Titan gazing at the field
Where rest the tokens of a hard-won strife,
Then marching on his proud, triumphal course,
Whose splender mocks the victims of his might.
I could not faint, nor sleep, nor dream, nor die;
Only from out the stupor which had wrapp'd
Each limb and feeling after anguish fierce,

My glaring eyes still watch'd that cruel sun,
Till each red ball seem'd living orbs of flame;
And yet I could not move them from the sky,
Or turn aside my weary, heavy head;
And on my bosom lay that young, fair brow,
Stirless and pale, and wreathed with clustering curls,
Whose golden beauty seem'd like halo bright,
His glory's crown won ere his Heaven was reach'd;
Still press'd the lovely head upon my heart,
Till vivid fancy pictured it a world,
That greater grew with each half-stifled breath,
Until my frame seem'd whelm'd beneath the mass;
And once, when as his pale lips murmur'd out
With fleeting sigh one passionate, sweet tone,
The holiest, tenderest word,—a mother's name,—
Methought an earthquake, with swift, sudden shock,
Had wreck'd the stillness of my forced repose.
I strove to cast my crushing burden off,
But could not move a muscle of my form;
I would have raved, but that my swollen tongue
Lay parch'd and blacken'd in my panting mouth,
Like some dead thing, without the power to move.
Visions of hideous shape o'er-rode my mind;
The boy's soft ringlets each seem'd serpent-coils!
The clinging fingers, but a monster's grasp!
And every grain of sand, a living sting!
My brain was bursting! how I wish'd for death,
As madness slowly banish'd longing thought,—
For I was nearly mad!

But, hark! a shout!
The hasty tramp of many coming feet!
The sound of human voices! and, oh, joy!
The flash of water on my spell-bound sight!

Another caravan, whose ampler store
Had borne them safely o'er their desert route,
Had sought for ours,—urged onward by the bones
And speechless dead that mark'd our frantic course,
To save the few, and found its remnant,—me,—
Yes,—only me! The angel in my arms
Had look'd farewell, and wing'd its homeward flight,
E'en as the messengers of hope restored
My flying reason to its tottering throne!

1856.

THE LEGEND OF ERROL.

THE watch-dog whined the whole long night,
The wind went wailing past;
Strange voices fill'd the castle-halls,
Strange shriekings swell'd the blast;
The firelight flickering on the hearth
Made shadows on the wall;
But mid the chamber's fearful gloom
Seem'd other shades to fall!

From off the large and massive bed
  Was drawn each curtain-fold,
Where lay a shrouded, stiffening form,
  That scarcely yet was cold:
The Miser of the Manor there,
  Whose path the bairns would shun,
Had died with twilight's fading hues,
  Beloved and blest by none!

Within the wide, black chimney-place
  The ruddy blaze burn'd bright:
'Twas many a year since that dark room
  Had known so rare a sight!
And crouch'd upon a little stool
  Beside the fitful flame,
With skinny hands and shaking head,
  There sat an aged dame!

An arm-chair, deep and high and worn,
  Held one as angels fair,
But half a child, with snowy dress
  And shining, golden hair,—
The old man's niece,—the Ladye Maude,
  The last of that proud race:
How ever came from such a stock
  A flower so full of grace?

And hovering o'er the embers red,
  As lull'd the wind's sad wail,
That palsied hag, in solemn tones,
  Told some unearthly tale

Of startling omens, potent spells,
  Of graves at midnight robb'd,
Of trance-bound sleep, and buried forms
  Wherein the life still throbb'd.

The Ladye Maude grew pale with fear,
  Her eyes grew wild with dread,
Thus listening to that toothless crone,
  Thus looking on the dead;
She could not move a single limb,
  But sat with lips apart,
And hands tight clasp'd upon her breast
  To still her beating heart.

The clock struck twelve; her blood ran cold,
  As rang day's solemn knell,
And on her soul with each slow stroke
  A greater terror fell;
For, as each echo sank away,
  The weird witch at her knee
An incantation chanted low,
  Of ancient glamourie!

A wild idea fill'd her brain,
  And stopp'd her smother'd breath;
She deem'd that mystic summons woke
  The ghastly ranks of Death;
She thought the corpse rose from its bed
  And trod with muffled feet;
The firelight through the shadowy gloom
  Waved like a winding-sheet!

A sudden shudder broke the spell;
  Then, nerved with frenzied might,
She shrieking rush'd through those dark halls
  Out in the cold, bleak night,
And left that wither'd demon there
  To keep her watch alone,
To hide the miser's stolen gold
  Beneath the broad hearthstone!

The banner'd flagstaff crashing fell
  Mid newly waken'd blast;
The mastiff ceased his warning howl
  As that slight figure pass'd;
And one who, sleepless, saw the storm
  That gather'd in the sky,
Long after told, in humble homes,
  How flew that vision by!

Loch Errol's falls were white with spray,
  Loch Errol lay below;
The rough rocks on Loch Errol's side
  Were veil'd in stainless snow;
And, pure as that unsullied snow
  Fresh from its cloudy home,
A fair thing slept at morning's dawn
  Amid Loch Errol's foam!

With arms entwined with golden hair,
  And cross'd on stirless breast,
She floated on Loch Errol's wave,
  Unheeding its unrest;

The bride of Death, in white array'd,
With childish, angel face,
Loch Errol bore to Heaven's gate
The last of Errol's race!

LAUREL HILL.

In this cemetery, situated a few miles from Philadelphia, are deposited the mortal remains of Joseph C. Neal, over whose last resting-place a beautiful and emblematic monument has been erected to his memory, by friends "who had loved him as a man and admired him as an author."

WITH chasten'd spirit wandering mid the graves,
I pass'd an hour afar from worldly sound,
Where earthly care no longer Toil enslaves,
Where silence only, and Death's types, abound.

The soothing stillness of the summer air,
The waving trees that shadow'd sculptured stone,
The unknown names of those who moulder'd there,
Subdued my soul like music's solemn tone.

I mark'd the token that Affection rears
Above the buried dust so loved in life;
Where fragrant flowers, nursed by Sorrow's tears,
Adorn the sod where rests a child or wife;

And paused a moment by a lonely spot,
The unrecorded mound wherein may sleep
Some nameless waif, whose unremember'd lot
Found naught to hope and left no friend to weep.

How many minds unconquer'd by their fate,
How many brains that throbb'd with feverish thought,
How many wordless yearnings for the great,
Have found beyond this bourn the goal they sought!

What garner'd wisdom, what unwritten lore,
What glowing visions, and what noble worth,
Have shone unvalued, then dropp'd back once more
Like unset jewels into mines of earth!

Here stately monuments of graceful art
Proclaim the virtues of the flatter'd dead:
How oft an epitaph exalts a heart
Whose deeds no lustre on its life-time shed!

Yet here, apart, mid calm, sequester'd glade,
A pathway winds, by pilgrim homage worn,
Where generous Love and Friendship's tasteful aid
Have shrined the relics whose repose they mourn.

Rough from the quarry hewn, in shapeless grace
Th' unpolish'd block of virgin marble stands,
And forms the massive but unmodell'd base
Where chisell'd urn admiring praise commands.

Expressive symbol of the mind unwrought,
Till Time to Labor's work perfection brings,
And kindred souls, fulfilling Nature's thought,
Undying laurels carve where ivy clings.

'Twas minstrel's truest type, that needs no words,
The stringless lyre leaning on thy grave!
Death early loosed thy spirit's "silver chords,"
And still'd the music that thy being gave.

Yet Hope's proud dreams might ask no more of Fame
Than such a tribute for an honor'd tomb,
Where tears of grief bedew the cherish'd name,
And glory spreads her bays of fadeless bloom!

THE OLD GUARD AT WATERLOO.

"La Garde Impériale meurt, mais ne se rend pas!"

They were as "giants on the earth," those demigods of France,
When their chieftain gave the signal for their eagles to advance;
For they knew their columns ever led the fortune of the day,
And where their standard floated was the thickest of the fray!

Their comrades fell before their eyes, crush'd by the iron rain,—
They trampled on their prostrate forms, and fill'd the ranks again!
No time to grieve o'er loved ones then, no time for tears to flow!
They only dream'd of glory's wreath, their monarch, and the foe!

All Europe trembled as they march'd, their only music, groans;
For on their storied valor hung the safety of her thrones!
With stern, unfaltering footsteps they trod that dreadful field,
Their motto graven on their minds,—to die, but not to yield!

Mid the roaring of the cannon, amid the flash of swords,
Arose from falling warriors these dauntless, noble words!
Their gaping wounds were ruddy, they fought mid waves of blood,
But the "Old Guard" yielded never, and each died where he stood!

What cared they that each onward step was nearer to the grave,
When at their head rode fearless Ney, the bravest of the brave?

These victors of unnumber'd fights braved death
without a sigh;
What reck'd these heroes where they fell, if th'
Emperor saw them die?

Napoleon! how they loved that name, their pride
in peace or war!
That sound baptized in bloody shrines, full many a
ghastly scar!
Its echoes rang from Lodi's bridge through every
age and land;
It lived within the hearts and deeds of this adoring
band!

As faster flew the countless shot, they fell by hundreds
then;
Yet steady and unbroken stood that square of
valiant men!
For when balls and charging squadrons some fatal
breach had made,
They, fighting, wheel'd, and form'd again, as though
upon parade!

Their very foes look'd on amazed to see such desperate
strife,
And sent a messenger to stay this reckless loss of
life,—
To summon these proud veterans to acknowledge
their defeat;
But they shouted, "Vive Napoléon!" and perish'd
at his feet!

Cambronne, their leader, struggled still amid a bleeding few,
The last of all the brilliant host that went to Waterloo!
The Allies ceased their murderous fire, the day was nearly done,
When their herald bade him render up the glory he had won!

The warrior rear'd his wounded form, and, glancing proudly round,
He pointed with his crimson'd blade where dead men heap'd the ground;
Then rang above the battle-plain the world-renown'd reply,
"The Old Guard ne'er surrender; the Old Guard only die!"

And thus they pass'd invincible, unvanquish'd save by Death,
Napoleon in their dying thought and on their latest breath.
They sprang to birth at his command, they vanish'd with his fall,
As sunbeams always rise and set around their parent-ball.

NAPOLEON'S LEGACY.

Shortly before his death, the Emperor was asked by Madame Bertrand, under whose protection he wished to leave his son. "I will leave my son under the protection of the French Army!" was the reply.

THERE, on the captive's barren rock,
  Imprison'd by the sea,
The great man's heart bequeth'd to France
  A precious legacy.
No countless store of hidden gold,
  No secret worth a throne,
No priceless gem of sacred Art:—
  These were no more his own!
He left no crowns for traitor brows,
  No lands his sword had won:
A nobler trust was thine, fair France,—
  His darling, only son!

Not from the Bourbon line of kings,
  Not from the fickle crowd,
Not from the courtier train that once
  Before his glory bow'd,
Not from the haughty Fleur de Lis,
  O'er humbled Gallia flung,
The chain'd and dying lion sought
  Protection for his young!

But to the army he had loved—
  The Legion of the Brave,
The veterans of a hundred fields—
  This solemn charge he gave!

'Twas to the eagles he had rear'd
  In Alpine eyries high,
And train'd "the Sun of Austerlitz"
  To face with fearless eye!
To whom he gave his sad embrace
  At Fontainebleau's review,
And only saw their proud wings droop
  At stormy Waterloo!
'Twas but to these Napoleon left
  His dearest, last bequest,
To guard their chieftain's child when he,
  The sire, should be at rest!

O warriors of the Empire,
  What answer shall ye make
To the well-known form that waits ye
  By Acheron's dark lake?
Will ye point to old Vienna,
  Who saw his conquests there,
And bid him seek mid kindred foes
  His kingdom's crownless heir?
Oh, little worth the monarch's trust
  In these, the tried and brave,
Who, living, left Napoleon's son
  To fill a captive's grave!

THE WORLD AND THE DREAMER.

"Up and be doing!" cries the busy world,
  Forever hastening to a golden goal:
"Why sitt'st thou idle thus, with folded hands,
  While all around thee tides of action roll?
Labor to live! and live alone for work!
  This is man's destiny! Come, take thy share!
Cast off the sloth of visions! murder dreams!
  He conquers most whose will the most shall
    dare!"

Brave words, O world! I hear their cheerful tones,
  And raise my looks where strives thy restless
    throng,
Where Wealth and Power tread o'er prostrate necks,
  Where Right falls wearied 'neath the blows of
    Wrong!
I see the many panting in the race
  Up Gain's steep hill, with glittering baubles strewn,
Toil, fail, and sink, spurn'd downward by the few
  Who smile at suffering from self's guilt-won
    throne!

I list the music of thy ceaseless work,
  The anvil's sound, the steam-king's mighty breath,
The march of eager feet through learning's road.
  And Triumph's song of names unknown to Death!

Yet hear above the chorus of thy strain
  The echoes which have fill'd each age of time,—
The groans of serfs, the shrieks of martyr'd faith,
  Oppression's shout o'er Freedom slain by crime!

I will not enter mid thy wild unrest,
  Nor bind my thoughts on Custom's grinding wheel,
Nor cringe to tyrant Pride, though purple-robed,
  Nor yield my new-born dreams to Action's steel!
God feeds my soul on visions, as of yore
  He fill'd his chosen ones with heavenly bread:
And shall I scorn this manna of the skies,
  To be, like them, on earthly viands fed?

Pass on, O world: we have our separate paths:—
  Thou to the busy battle-field of life,
The dreamer, I, to stay apart with peace
  And mark the currents of thy endless strife!
But mind shall labor, though my life be still,
  My soul be brave, although my armor rust;
And e'en thy warriors yet may turn aside
  To hold communion with my sleeping dust!

THE UNWRITTEN ELEGY.

Shelley, whose Elegy on Keats is one of the most exquisite poems in the English language, has yet to receive the same homage to his own genius.

HAS no one writ thine Elegy,
Bard of a magic lyre,—
Whose subtle music thrills high souls
With more than transient fire,—
Whose dreamy tenderness of song,
And delicate, rich tone,
Might win a wandering Peri's voice
To make the strain its own?

Has no one writ thine Elegy?—
No mourner at thy tomb
Cast down a single fadeless flower
To decorate its gloom?
Not one ambitious minstrel-hand
To snatch a leaf of fame
To shine amid th' immortal light
Reflected from thy name?

Has no one writ thine Elegy,—
Whose eloquence of woe
Could o'er the broken-hearted dead
In such deep pathos flow,

That even they whose cruel scorn
  The poison'd arrow sent
Have wept o'er Adonais' bier,
  Subdued by Love's Lament?

Has no one writ thine Elegy,—
  Whose spirit scaled the skies
Upon the ladder of sweet sounds
  The lark rears as she flies,—
Who claim'd companionship with clouds,
  And, like their sparkling dew,
Whose freshening thoughts made many a flower
  Of life spring up anew?

Has no one writ thine Elegy,—
  Whose clear and brilliant mind
Had rent with fearless hand the veil
  That Custom's minions bind
Upon the shining brow of Truth
  To hide her glory's rays,
Then never from her halo's glow
  Turn'd back thine earnest gaze?

Has no one writ thine Elegy,—
  Who trod with reverent feet
Mid Nature's praise-resounding aisles,
  Where man and mystéries meet,—
Who found in forest, mount, or sea
  Thy soul's unending feast,
Till symphonies of ringing words
  Proclaim'd Creation's Priest?

Has no one writ thine Elegy,—
  Not even he whose hand
Unto thy classic funeral pyre
  Applied the kindling brand,—
Whose poet-soul had shared with thine
  The scorns and wounds of Fate,
And e'en whose last libation pour'd
  To Friendship waken'd Hate!

Has no one writ thine Elegy,—
  None of thy kindred band?
Ho! Master Singers of the world!
  Ho! Bards of every land!
Ho! ye whose words have sway'd the throng
  When echoed from his lute!
Because the nightingale is still,
  Are other warblers mute?

Will no one write his Elegy?—
  Come, gather round his urn,
And each, like Magi at a shrine,
  His share of incense burn!
What nobler, prouder theme than this
  Can human purpose find,
On which to string your gems of thought,
  Ye monarchs of the mind?

Will no one write his Elegy?—
  O Laureate of a throne,
Forget the scenes of ages fled:
  Immortalize thine own!

From "Morte d'Arthur" turn thy dreams
  To that one grave at Rome,
Till floats o'er England's modern dead
  A requiem from home!

Will no one write his Elegy?—
  Unsung his ashes wait
The tribute which the bard alone
  Can render to the great.
Then hasten, troubadours of earth,
  Thy gifts of song to bring,
Till unto Shelley's name all hearts
  In answering echoes ring!

1857.

BORN.

A REQUIEM and a jubilee!
  An infant born, a mother dead!
A storm without, a wail within!
  A starless heaven overhead!
A father's half-averted eye!
  Hot tears above a white robe shed!
A flickering firelight in the room,
Strange shadows swaying mid the gloom,
A broken flower, a bud's fresh bloom,
A life that wrought its giver's doom!

Thus welcomed in an ominous hour,
  A new soul waken'd on the earth,
With snow and hail on striving winds;
  With death and sorrow on the hearth!
What fate is hid in coming years
  Thus heralded by such a birth?
A loveless childhood, wild and lone!
A youth of yearnings crush'd, unknown!
A heart with idols overthrown!
A woman's lot! Moan, baby, moan!

DEAD.

Dead!
The damp, dark mould enwraps her form;
  The eyes are darken'd evermore;
The pallid hands hold wither'd buds;
  Dust gathers where was bloom before.
  Life's joys, life's hopes, life's tears are o'er;
    For she is dead!

Dead!
The grave is Lethe for all care:
  There dwells the peace her years knew not;
Regrets are hush'd, remorse is still:
  Her very love will be forgot
  By those who shared her shaded lot;
    For she is dead!

Dead!
One stands beside the sculptured tomb,
And reads her name upon the stone:
In youth's proud hour she crush'd his dreams;
And yet he comes, the last, alone,
To weep for her was ne'er his own
Till she was dead!

Dead!
A stranger fills her place at home;
The weeds grow thick around her grave:
One plucks a flower from the sod
That henceforth over land and wave
Will throb on heart that faithful gave
Love strong as Death!

THE SAINT-ESPRIT.

The Saint-Esprit, or Flower of the Holy Ghost, is the small blossom of an air-plant, so called from the striking resemblance in its appearance to that of a dove with half-closed wings sitting in the cup of a lily.

Afar on the waves of the blue Southern Ocean,
Like a beauty asleep on her lover's fond breast,
Lies the fairest of isles, while the sea's fond emotion
Swells in billowy kisses that brighten her rest.

For no water that rolls has foam-crest so golden
As these sun-lighted pulses that throb on her shore;
And no sage has e'er dream'd over mysteries so olden
As that fathomless deep could to ages restore.
And 'tis murmuring now, mid its love's wild embracing,
Some rare legend to waken the silence of morn,
While on scent-laden wings of the winds, that are chasing
Our snowy-sail'd bark, the sweet echoes are borne!

Encircled by hills, a lone valley is hidden
In the midst of this isle, still untrodden by man,—
An emblem of Eden ere its fruit was forbidden,
Ere humanity's sin or creation began!
Like some fleet, graceful Almée who wreathes, as she dances,
Her many-hued scarf mid her loose, shining hair,
Then, bounding away from the slaves she entrances,
To a couch strewn with blossoms, sinks breathlessly there!
Thus a spray-spangled stream, through the mossy rocks winding,
Leaps suddenly down, with a gay, mocking tone,
The rainbow-dyes still mid its foam-tresses binding,

As it falls in a lake of queen-lilies the throne!
Like armies of giants renown'd in old stories,
Here forests primeval spread their evergreen glades,

Where birds with the plumage of sunsetting glories
Are sparkling like jewels mid the dim, dusky shades,
Or warbling like Peris through Paradise straying,
Till with rapturous music the green arches ring,
While their leaf-hidden nests are gracefully swaying
On the wild, fragrant vines that so tenderly cling
Round these veterans of nature, their branches entwining,
Till a labyrinth of verdure o'er-roofs all the scene,
And the brightness of day, in scatter'd beams shining,
Makes a network below of shadow and sheen!

And here 'mong the parasite plants that embower
The aisles of a temple whose sole incense is song,
There blossoms, air-nurtured, a delicate flower,
Round whose marvellous beauty rare fancies may throng!
In days that have vanish'd, there stood by the river
That rolls through the Orient its world-hallow'd wave,
The Christ clothed in manhood mankind to deliver,
And John the Baptizer, with warning to save!
When, lo! from the cloud o'er the holy group bending,
Floats the Spirit of God, in the form of a dove,
And there on the head of the Saviour descending
Lights a token of purity, promise, and love!

Soon their steps from the shores of the Jordan
retreating,
The Prophet and Lord journey onward to die;
While the messenger-dove, its mission completing,
Its spotless wings spreads, o'er the wide world to
fly!
But where on this earth shall the heaven-born rover
Find a home all unsullied by traces of sin,
A shelter still guileless and worthy to cover
The pure breast that late harbor'd God's Spirit
within?
It floats o'er the wilderness, sails o'er the mountain,
Skims the rivers and lakes, resting noonday nor
night,
Or longingly lingers by some wild-wood or fountain;
But the taint of man's presence still urges its
flight!

Its pinions, still stainless, had ceased not their
motion
Since they soar'd from the halo on His holy head,
Till over this isle in the far Southern Ocean,
Its pilgrimage ended, their flutterings are led,
Where, wheeling mid trees that through clouds
seem to tower,
It slowly sinks down, seeking refuge and rest,
Till at last the lily-leaved cup of this flower
Spreads a velvety couch for its white, weary breast;
And, with plumage half folded, it silently slumbers,
Now forever a part of this blossom so rare,

While, harp-like, its tendrils vibrate with the numbers
Of melodies rich that the winds waken there!

Its seeds, like the feathers of birds that are flying,
Float away, and find root in the soft, stirring breeze,
That evermore thus near the waterfall sighing
Drapes the forest around with entwined Saint-Esprits,
Till the dark, shady woods are white with the glory
Of flowers untainted by contact with earth,
While the foam-crested waves repeat the strange story
Of this wonderful nestling of heavenly birth!
Thus murmur'd the Sea, mid its love's wild embracing,
This new legend to waken the silence of morn,
And on scent-laden wings of the wind, that was chasing
Our snowy-sail'd bark, the faint echoes were borne!

AN OLD STORY.

Once on an autumn day, in bygone years,
Two lovers stood beside a lonely grave;
And, as they read the story on the stone,
Both throbbing hearts a sigh of sorrow gave.

'Twas sad,—that record of an ended life:
  It told of one, a woman young and fair,
Who sprang to meet the glory of her spring,
  Then brought its faded, storm-crush'd blossoms
    there!
She loved, and died; and o'er her shrouded form
  The heavy sods lay black and damp and cold,
While crimson leaves, like her own glowing hopes,
  Were falling thick, and mingling with the mould!

They read, and gazed into each other's eyes;
  Then spake the girl half sadly through her tears:—
"And is this all that life can give to love,
  And all that love accords to patient years?
Rest for the wearied and broken heart,
  And grave where only strangers stop to weep?
And yet perchance 'twere better thus to lose,
  Amid the dreamless quiet of death's sleep,
The bitter knowledge of affection lost,
  Than live to mourn youth's perish'd love and
    faith
My own beloved, should such fate e'er be mine,
  Pray God mine too may be an early death!"

He still'd her new-born fear with tender words,
  And swore, beside the stranger's warning tomb,
That Time should ne'er his fervent truth destroy,
  And bade her chase her brow's prophetic gloom!
She was but woman: so, with yearning heart,
  She wept and listen'd, smiled and still believed;

And arm in arm they turn'd from that sad mound,
Forgetting all the thought that there had grieved!—
But when the autumn leaves had changed their shade
Once more from glossy green to falling gold,
Their fading glories deck'd another grave,
And she was young who shared that couch of mould!

PRAYER AT THE POLE.

"Just before we started [on the return with the rescued men], while the rest of the party surrounded the sledge, Dr. Kane rendered thanks to the Great Ruler of human destinies for the goodness He had evinced in preserving our feeble lives while struggling over the ice desert, exposed to a blast almost as withering as that from a furnace. The scene was exceedingly solemn, as, deeply impressed by our situation, our commander poured forth ready and eloquent sentences of gratitude in that lonely solitude, whose scenery offered every thing to depress the mind, nothing to cheer it. Not a word fell from his lips that did not find a response in our hearts, when we reflected upon the dangers we had undergone, and the certainty of death which would have followed a continuance of exposure for even a few hours."—(Quoted from the Narrative of Wilson in Dr. Elder's "Life of Kane.")

A LITTLE group of worn-out men,
With weary limbs and shatter'd forms,
Whose stalwart wills and gallant hearts
Were strong to face dark danger's storms!

And one amidst them, slight of frame,
  And pale from strife with death and pain,
A hero's soul, whose martyr zeal
  Bore nobly suffering's cankering chain!

They met within the solemn aisles
  Of ice-built shrine, a temple grand,
Alone upon a frozen sea,
  The saving and the rescued band,
Mid crystal columns rear'd aloft
  Against a gray and cloud-draped dome,—
The only thing—that shadow'd sky—
  In all the waste that look'd like home!

They stood with bow'd, uncover'd heads,
  With reverent mien and moisten'd eyes,
Remembering scenes that long had pass'd,
  Recalling love's most tender ties,
As softly on the keen, cold air
  Their leader's voice rose calm and clear,
And raised, like prophet's tone, the hope
  That in each heart had found a bier.

Few words of humble, grateful praise,
  For guidance, life, and rest, a prayer,
A low "Amen" from quivering lips,
  Were all the pomps of service there!
It gave them strength to conquer death;
  It made them brave to dare and do;
It kept them faithful to the end,
  A band of brothers, tried and true!

Then bless them, souls of Christian men
  O'er all the earth who praise and pray;
And bless *him* most of all, their chief,
  Who first in duty led the way,—
Who first upon those regions drear
  Of frozen, unknown waters spoke
The name of Christ, whose world-bless'd sound
  The solitude of silence broke!

Those polar mounts of ice may melt
  Beneath the Arctic's summer skies;
May speed the nations' hoarded wealth,
  And 'neath the tropics ebb and rise;
Yet bear abroad, where'er they flow,
  That baptism of the holy Name
They echoed from *his* voice who died
  And left those bergs to spread his fame!

1858.

ONE LIFE.

Low and lone in the church-yard corner
  Is a grave we saw not before:
There's one who was restless and erring,
  Will weary on earth nevermore!
There are feet that have ceased from straying
  In paths of folly and shame,
Red lips that the white worms are kissing,
  An unwept and unhonor'd name!

She had youth and beauty and fancy,
  She had passions, tempting, and sin,
She laugh'd loudest at reckless revels,
  While her heavy heart wept within;
She fetter'd all men with her glances,
  She thrill'd them with touch of her hand;
She was fairest and highest and lowest
  Of the city's Cyprian band!

There were those who scorn'd her for sinning,
  Who "pass'd by on the other side,"
Who shunn'd her as one that was leprous,
  Unclean to their purified pride,
Who vetoed with sceptres of virtue
  Her claims upon sympathy's care,
Who frown'd on her dawning repentance,
  Or blush'd her back into despair!

Her heart was the heart of a woman,
  And her soul was a human soul;
She had feelings, yearnings, and trials,
  And a name for God's judgment-roll!
It may be, in some soften'd moment,
  Love's sisterly, winning tone
May have guided her steps from evil,
  Till they paused by the great white throne!

She heard not the calls that were murmur'd
  By those standing off and apart:
So she laugh'd defiance at preachers,
  And strangled the pain in her heart!

And she died, society's outcast;
  But perchance, mid her life of shame,
Some charities secret and precious
  In heaven have whiten'd her name!

CALLS AND RESPONSES.

"Poet, uplifting thy soft, earnest eyes,
  Looking with lofty rapture o'er the earth,
What thinkest thou of this, the wondrous sphere
  Whereon thy strain melodious had birth?"

"Earth is the mother of the Beautiful,
  And wears new glories every passing day;
My soul grows drunken with her loveliness,
  And longs forever mid her wealth to stay;
My song interprets then to colder hearts
  The mighty mysteries of her wordless tone,
And, priest-like chanting through the temple-aisles,
  Leads up the people to the Maker's throne."

"True, Beauty's worshipper, thy world *is* fair,
  But should be loved because 'tis sacred too;
For God's own feet have trod its precious soil:
  Jehovah hallow'd earth by passing through."

"Philosopher, who countest heaven's bright orbs,
  Thou lonely watcher of the moonlight night,

What seems to thee this planet of our own,
Whereon thy sense first saw the morn's rich light?"

"Earth moves upon her orbit in the skies,
A mite mid space, and yet a shining star,
Whereon all other constellations gaze,
And hail a sister in this speck afar.
And thus the lore which Eastern Magi taught
Of suns and systems fills this heart of mine,
Where evermore those distant, glowing lights
Shed o'er life's trial-storms a peace divine."

"Yet should they lift thy soul with purer joy,
Joy that the Orient sages never felt,
That, mid these myriads of brighter worlds,
On thine alone God the Redeemer dwelt!"

"O weeper, sorrowing over broken hopes,
Who seest all things through a veil of tears,
Forget a little while thy mournful past;
Say how to thee thy parent globe appears."

"Earth spread before the vision of my youth
A vast, sweet garden fill'd with fragrant flowers.
Time taught me soon each blossom hid a thorn,
And pain repaid the bliss of happy hours.
Now look I forth, and see rare glories still,
Yet know the sting that lurks 'neath every prize;
And so, mid earth's green fields and clustering fruit,
My anguish'd spirit faint with sorrow lies!"

"'Twas in the *Garden* of Gethsemane
 Christ's agony and sweat of blood were borne:
The brows that bend 'neath weight of human cross
 Wear never laurel, but are crown'd with thorn."

Sage, singer, sufferer, *man*, whate'er thou art,
 Look proudly forth across this world of thine,
And glory in thy grand humanity:
 'Twas made in image of the One Divine!
'Tis higher, too, than highest angel forms;
 For ours, not theirs, the nature that was ta'en,
When sinless Jesus died like mortal man,
 And soar'd in human form to heaven again!
And love thy earth; 'tis sanctified for time,
 Since she has held dead Christ within her breast.
These, moulds of dust, should make thy noblest pride,
 Since most in these thou and thy earth were blest.

THE QUESTION.

An angel ever stands
 Beside the portals barr'd
 Where spirits enter in
 The kingdom of the King,
 Enfranchised of their sin.

He holds within his hands
The book of human fate,
Wherein he marks each name
With signs that seraphs know
Of glory or of shame.

For 'tis his solemn place
To ask the newly dead
Who seek for entrance there,
The question which decides
Their bliss or their despair.
Before his shining face
But truth can stand unveil'd;
And all that hear his tone
Must answer justly then,
Uncounsell'd and alone.

That angel will not ask,
"What money hast thou won?
What conquests hast thou made?
What pleasure hast thou gain'd?
What homage hast thou paid?"
No! his is sterner task:
The words that he will say
Will quell each trembling soul,
Will waken mortal fear,
Reviewing memory's roll.

"What hast thou done with time?"
Thus will the angel speak;—
"What of thy days of life,

Returning nevermore,
With good or evil rife?
Time lost is man's worst crime:
Well spent, it is the key
That opens heaven's gate.
Art worthy? or hast found
Time's value all too late?"

What hast thou done with time?
Ponder it, fellow-man;
Think of it, dust of earth:
God lends thee time till death;
'Tis borrow'd at thy birth.
What hast thou done with time?
When hours of breath are o'er,
Canst answer, "Faithful, Lord,"
And see the gates of pearl
Unclose before the word?

DIED YOUNG.

Died young! About those little, common words
A mournful cadence ever seems to cling,
Like echoes of a broken song, that still
A sense of yearning to our spirits bring.

Died young! The living who remain grow gray,
And yet these dead stand in our memories' light,
Unwither'd, fresh, untouch'd by time and care,
Or glorified, perchance, by faith's fond sight.

Died young! We think of them too oft as fruit
Blighted by frost before the ripening hour,
Or with a selfish pain that on our path
Should fade the beauty of an opening flower.

Died young! They have escaped so much of sin,
So much of sorrow, and such stings of shame,
That gratitude should mingle with our grief,
Knowing these dear ones kept their youth's pure name.

Died young! They had not lost their eager hope,
Their glad, first trust in all that seemeth fair,
The power to dream, to revel in romance,
Or bring a guileless soul to God in prayer.

Died young! Experience had never torn
The roseate veil from Nature's face away,
Forced tears for perish'd loves and friendships slain,
Or shown them that their idols were of clay.

Died young! They left the bitterness of life,
Uncrown'd with thorns, unwearied by the cross;
And, if we miss them on our own bleak road,
To us, to us alone comes thought of loss!

Died young! Leap'd warm into the vale of death,
Which we with solemn step shall one day tread,
And then, dear friends grown old with this world's ill,
We meet our youth again, with earth's young dead!

AGNES.

The fading glory of an autumn day
Flash'd through the west, then died to dusk away,
Its red beams lingering, in a quaint old room,
On two that noted not the gathering gloom.

For they were lovers. She had yielded all,
Hope, faith, and dreams, unto his passion's thrall;
They both were young and fair, nor yet had seen
The freshness vanish from youth's early green!

His arms were round her; like a fluttering dove,
Her heart was folded in its nest of love;
Her swimming eyes gazed up into his own,
Meeting the wordless thoughts that there, too, shone.

The world was nought to them: their love was life;
Each passing moment was with memories rife;
And, as his hand play'd fondly mid her hair,
He pictured forth the home they both should share.

Drawing her blushing brow upon his breast,
His quivering lips then on her own he press'd,
Murmuring in broken accents, all the while,
How all through life his light should be her smile.

And both were happy,—in each other's eyes
Watching the love-light art can ne'er disguise;
A moment heedless of th' impending cloud
Whose shadow soon their future must enshroud.

For they were parting,—he to seek once more
His distant home upon another shore,
And she to mourn in solitude and tears
O'er time's slow march, affection's tender fears.

He held her long in one close, wild embrace,
Both trembling on each other's brow to trace
The passing semblance of a bitter dread
Lest absence on their love some change should shed.

Her sudden sobs the boding silence broke,
While he in passion's whisper'd accents spoke:—
"Dearest, I love thee,—love but only thee:
Thou art the star that guides my destiny!

"My best beloved, I will return once more,
And then—and then—our partings will be o'er!
I will be true as though still at thy side,—
True as if thou wert all my own, my bride!"

Slowly she calm'd the tumult of her tears,
And cast aside the memory of her fears,
Answering, with trust unfaltering, "I too
Will be forever faithful, ever true!"

Once more their bursting hearts together beat,
Once more their lips the parting kiss repeat;
And then, with one last look, he turn'd away,
Leaving her weeping mid her hopes to pray.

Her days moved slowly by, and grew to years,—
A sad procession calendar'd with tears,—
And yet he came not. Still unwed and fair,
She learned her woman's lot, a silent grief to bear!

For months his letters cheer'd her lonely way:
Oft read, caressed, they on her bosom lay,
To lighten every evil life could bring,
And hours of sunshine o'er her path to fling.

At length she saw a shade of coldness steal
Amid their warmth, no language could conceal:
She rent the veil of eloquence apart,
And read the naked truth with bleeding heart.

His life was brilliant; mid its busy tide,
That dream of tenderness was drown'd and died;
In gradual change his idol less became,
Till all remain'd was memory and a name!

He was not false,—but nature made him light;
His fancy roved to each thing new and bright;
And, deeming that he truly loved the while,
He watch'd the passion fade, with fickle smile.

She loved him,—loved as only women love,
Her thought of him all other thought above.
She saw her god lie shatter'd by a breath,
And crush'd with foot of pride her hopes to death!

The years pass'd on; and yet she still was young,
And fame upon her brows its bays had flung;
Fortune with gold had paved her triumph's road;
No trace of sorrow mid her beauty show'd!

And then he came. Upon that distant shore
Her glory reach'd him; and he longed once more,
With something of the olden love, to gaze
On her whose power had won a world-wide praise.

They met; and he, remembering, thought to see
The same slight girl *his* Agnes used to be,
With floating curls, and earnest, tender eyes,
And artless mien unspoil'd by worldly guise.

They met,—amid a ball-room's restless crowd.
With startled grace, as to a queen he bow'd.
"Surely," he mused, "that woman proud and gay
Cannot be her I parted from one day,—

"Cannot be her who wept upon my arm
In all the passion of love's fond alarm,—
Who clung to me, and press'd her lips to mine,
Murmuring, 'Beloved, I am only thine!'

"It is not true! *She* could not meet me so,
Without one mention of the long ago,
Without one change of color or of tone,
As though a stranger spoke to her alone.

"And yet 'tis she! Her smile is still the same,—
Her glorious smile,—and, better still, her name.
How like an empress born upon the throne
She sways the crowd that see but her alone!

"She shall be mine once more: she loved me then;
Methinks old love will win new love again.
Perchance she loves me yet: a woman's heart
Loves rarely twice; her love of life is part."

And so he stood beside her as of yore,
Talk'd low, look'd love, as oftentimes before.
She smiled for answer with a mien as cold
As though for her there were no days of old.

At length he spoke of that sad parting scene,
Recall'd the happy times that once had been,
His heart quick-beating with the hope to trace
Some sign of lingering love upon her face.

At last he ask'd her, "Dost remember, too,
Thy promised vow to be forever true?
I've sought in vain thine image to forget:
May hope still dream thou dost remember yet?"

She stood a moment like Nemesis crown'd
With all the glory of a vengeance found;
Then turn'd with laugh as silvery as song,
And with the shaft of scorn repaid her wrong:—

"True unto thee! I do remember now
What I had long forgot! Some foolish vow,
Made—was't to thee?—when head and heart were soft!
But vows, through life, are made and broken oft!

"I do recall a scene where love-sick youth
Swore to romantic girl eternal truth,
But had forgotten both the vow and swain:—
I've been betroth'd some dozen times since then!

"Didst think to find me scourged by memory's rod,
With all my life like Rome's old two-faced god,
Looking one way towards a bitter past,
While towards the other all my hopes were cast?

"Thou hast not learn'd, in all these years since fled,
Love is a hungry thing, and must be fed
With constant pleadings, hopes, prayers, dreams, and sighs,
Or else he fades away, and, starving, dies?

"'Tis strange that I, who practised my first spell
Of power and conquest upon thee so well,
Would still have this to teach, that absence e'er
Destroys and buries sentiment's despair!

"And now farewell! we shall not meet again:
To-morrow sees me dashing o'er the main.
Ponder my lesson! To thy love twice told
Perchance I yet may listen—when I'm old."

And thus again they parted,—he, to feel
A real, despairing love her vengeance seal;
To mourn his folly, and to curse his fate,
That, loving well at last, he loved too late.

And she—and she—the golden moon that night
Look'd down from heaven on a piteous sight:
A woman kneeling with dishevell'd hair,
And pallid lips that murmur'd misery's prayer.

She had with words her nobleness belied,
And borne her bravely 'neath her mask of pride;
But now, alone with sorrow and the past,
Her heart's deep wounds could bleed in tears at last.

"O God!" she cried, "have mercy! let me die!
Or quench these memories of the times gone by!
Let me not curse him for my hopeless life,
My ruin'd peace, my hours of midnight strife!

"And give me patience, O my God, to bear
This veil of calmness which my days must wear!
That he may never know the secret pain
That binds my soul with its resistless chain.

"And yet—and yet, O God, for my wreck'd youth,
My broken dreams, my constant, hidden truth,
Still keep my memory green within his heart,
To haunt his path of life, whence I depart!"

The morrow saw her speeding o'er the main;
Ne'er press'd her foot her native soil again;
Another land and other friends became
The willing donors of extended fame.

Yet Rumor brought him tidings of her fate,
Of homage render'd her by proud and great,
And how she moved among the courtly throng,
As one whose thoughts to higher things belong.

Yet knew he not that, ere at last she died,
Love conquer'd all those weary years of pride,
And that his name grew cold upon the breath
Whose blessing ended in the realms of death!

GRAVES BY THE WAY.

Slow and alone up Life's oft travell'd road,
Bearing a cross, a weary woman trode,
And reach'd the turning-place,
Then paused beneath her burden's heavy weight,
And, like one lingering near a closing gate,
Look'd back with earnest face;

Gazed yearning back with sadden'd eyes, that bore
The shadows of spent clouds, whose storms of yore
Had swept her travell'd way,—
Saw heaping there rich wrecks of lovely things,
Dead forms of wasted hours with folded wings,
And lilies soil'd with clay.

As o'er the cross that lean'd upon her breast
She eager bent, her crown's sharp thorns outpress'd
Blood-drops from each deep wound,
That chased her rapid tears' unheeded flow,
As o'er and o'er she counted, oft and slow,
Lone graves that mark'd the ground.

First far adown, where fell Life's morning light,
Rose, blossom-deck'd, upon her misty sight
A little mound of mould;
A new bud sever'd from its parent stem,
A jewel dropp'd from home's bright diadem,
And all the tale was told.

A gentle darling from the household gone,
A sweet-voiced warbler with the angels flown,
To form within the skies
The first dear link in Death's heart-coiling chain,
That bound her memory with its cankering pain
To shores where nothing dies.

And, farther on, another resting-place,
Where damask-roses wither'd in their grace
Within the yew's dark shade,

Whose solemn branches bow'd their mournful state
Beneath the tender ivy's clinging weight,
O'er asphodel-strewn glade.

A doe, dart-stricken by a gushing spring,
A pure white cygnet with death-drooping wing,
The sculptured marble bore;
For here, way-weary, quaff'd of Lethe's stream
Her girlhood's early friend, and dream'd a dream
From which she woke no more.

Between the rocks and sea, then, lone, apart,
A plane-tree show'd where slept a bleeding heart,
That Genius had crown'd
With emblem-wreath of lotus, intertwined
With bright-leaved amaranth, whose flowers wind
The dark, sad cypress round.

Low bent adown the pilgrim gazer's head;
For o'er the turf that hid the gifted dead,
O'ergrown with eglantine,
The carved device on fallen column shone
Of torch, whereon crush'd purple clusters thrown
Quench'd light with ruby wine.

Then changed the road from straight and level way
To crook'd paths, whose dark and miry clay
Still soil'd her robe with stains;
No mossy turf the sharp rocks now outspread,
The dusky clouds hung lowering overhead,
And shadow'd brightest plains.

Like heated iron burning on her heart
She felt her crucifix, for just apart,
    Through broken hawthorn hedge,
She saw two sepulchres together laid,
Whereon pale yellow leaves a pall had made,
    The coming winter's pledge;

Twin tombs, whereon were symboll'd in the stone
Each emblem-token of the Something gone
    From earth and buried there.
Dead amaryllis strew'd the grave of Pride;
A shatter'd anchor show'd where Hope had died
    In battle with Despair.

She wept o'er all these scenes with woman-woe,
Silent and patient, whose tears' swift flow
    Awoke no noisy groan;
But suddenly a shriek ran through the air,
As if her life's whole agony and care
    Found voice in that one tone.

The cross, scarce noted mid her memory's pain,
Slipp'd slowly down, from where it long had lain,
    Upon her weight-worn breast,
Striking, arm-stay'd, upon a wound scarce heal'd,
Just o'er the heart, from whence the blow unseal'd
    Red streams that dyed her vest.

The while her fainting sight could dimly see
A phantom rise from 'neath an aloe-tree,
    With drooping myrtle crown'd;

Whose spectral hands white poppies held enclosed,
Signs of the sleep wherein the heart reposed
Ere startled by that sound.

"Dear Love, dost live again?" she feebly said;
"I buried thee! methought that thou wert dead,
And conquer'd evermore!
Why comes this ghost to mock my bitter fate?
I deem'd, that day my soul grew desolate,
That all thy power was o'er."

"Thy love is dead," replied the fleeting shade;
"'Twas like yon aloe where its couch is made,
That blooms but once, then dies!
'Tis but thy fancy gives me passing life,
And haunting memory, with fond visions rife,
Thus mocks thy yearning sight!"

The shades had lengthen'd when once more she stood,
With hidden wound, in brave yet solemn mood,
Ready to journey on;
But ere again she pass'd upon her way,
That still untraced through unknown darkness lay,
She knelt beside the stone

That mark'd a new-made grave, that morn not there,—
And thus breathed forth her soul's most earnest prayer:
"God of the quick and dead,

With mercy guide me through my coming life,
As once, of old, through deserts and through strife
Thy people safe were led!

"As in the wilderness graves strew'd *their* way,
See, too, on my past road, where heaps of clay
Bury my dead from sight;
And grant, O Lord, to shine amid my lot,
Alone, heart-wounded, and by love forgot,
This ray of pillar'd light;

"That ne'er again Death's ghastly shape may sweep
Across my path, no more these poor eyes weep
O'er cherish'd graves to be.
Let me die first, ere those I love shall go,
To leave me madden'd by life's yearning woe!
O God, not them, but me!

"Here lies my perish'd youth that died to-day,
Earth's brightest thing forever fled away,
Ne'er to return again.
I mourn for it, last, saddest loss of all,
Believing through my years no more can fall
Such heavy, bitter rain.

"And yet—and yet, my God, I still implore
This one atonement for the griefs of yore,
To lighten this my cross:
Spare my beloved ones till myself be dead;
Strike me, O Lord, but let me never shed
More tears for mortal loss!"

Then o'er her rood white rose-wreaths she entwined,
Emblems of silence, that henceforth should bind
The woes her soul might bear,
Then, rising, gazed once more adown the Past,
And towards The Future's night one long look cast,
Then bravely enter'd there.

ORIGIN OF GEMS.

THE OPAL.

ONCE, ere man was, the gates of God's high heaven
Were closed; and round the throne a rumor rose
That the lost Lucifer and all his host,
Grown madden'd in their mighty home of fire
By distant echoes of the bliss once theirs,
Would strive again to win their former seats!
And so on either side the portals barr'd
Gabriel and Michael lean'd upon their swords,
With pinions trailing on the court of gold;
While stretching up the shore of Life's great stream
There thronged a myriad of shining wings,
The army of the Highest come to wage
Celestial war 'gainst evil and despair!
And, like the suns that fill the universe,
Each one was silent, and with glory ray'd,
And but the leaders changed a single smile,
Part pity, partly sorrow, and part scorn,

When up the blue their fallen brethren soar'd,
Still angel-like, yet scarr'd all o'er with sin,
With white wings soil'd and shadow'd brows un-
crown'd,
And each one bearing from the burning lake
A portion of its quenchless, blazing flame;
Which casting down before the stainless gate,
They stood apart, and waited till its might
Should burst each crystal hinge and entrance show.
But when upon the empyrean soil
At last the glowing fragments crashing fell,
The sons of God came swarming to the breach,
With blades of Truth, bless'd by the Eternal One,
And drove them, shrieking, to their lowest hell,
And left them bound to torments evermore,
By chains of memory and hopeless grief.
And as the conquering spirits winged their flight,
With glad hosannas of triumphant praise,
Back to the radiance of Jehovah's face,
The arch-seraph Gabriel paused to raise
The scatter'd remnants of the shatter'd pearl,
That still was flashing with unhallow'd light,
And cast them down upon the new-form'd earth;
Where evermore its lovely pureness keeps
Th' imprison'd splendor of that mystic fire.
And man, half angel and half demon, wears
The Opal, as an emblem of his soul.

1859.

DIAMONDS.

They stood just out of their lost Paradise,
Adam and the Mother of All Living,
Still backward gazing, and yet seeing naught
For flashing of the flaming swords that hid
The gates of Eden closed 'gainst man and time.
The world was wide,—*there* was their bridal home!
Earth's plants were many,—Eve's dear flowers were
there!
There had they seen the light, and talk'd with God,
And there, a sovereign o'er created things,
Had fearless watch'd the beasts which he had named,
The tameless lion and the untamed stag,
Come meekly crouching unto Adam's call.
Now these had grown a terror or a grief,
The earth was cursed, and the death-angel born!
And, half afraid to face their future fate,
They linger'd yet around the cherish'd spot,
Each clinging to the other with such love,
Yet weeping with such passionate, sad woe,
That the bright angels guarding its lone paths
Bow'd down their radiant and light-crown'd heads,
And shed great tears of pity for their lot,
That, falling, roll'd adown the glowing swords,
And caught their brightness ere they sparkling fell;
Which Satan, wearing now his seraph-shape,
Did gather ere they touch'd th' illumined soil,—
Albeit that the precious drops became
Hard, shining stones within his fatal grasp,—

And offer'd them to Eve with mocking laugh,
Telling her she might buy a world of slaves
With those fair things, or reign, like queen-like night
Bedeck'd with stars, o'er every mortal hope,
If she would bind them on her perfect brow.
She listen'd not, nor knew the angels wept,
But, casting one long look from Adam's breast
Towards her bower of past bliss, bless'd God
That Love was left them still; then hand in hand
They turn'd away from Eden evermore.
And then the Tempter cast the glittering gems
Into the rivers that from thenceforth flow,
And bade them bear his malison to men;
And, as one woman heeded not their power,
All women else should yield them to their sway,
And Diamonds tempt the loveliest Eves on earth
To fancied Edens and to flaming swords.

RUBIES.

Abel was dead, and all the shuddering earth
Grew still before the awful voice of wrath,
That thrill'd the angels at the stern demand,
"Where is thy brother, Cain?" and Cain uprose
From gazing on the dead man's pallid face
With the great terror of a first remorse,
And trembled when he saw the solid ground
Oped not to hide his deed and him from God:
Then heard with sullen fear his future doom,

And dared to plead for life with that great Judge:
"All men will seek to slay me as I flee,
Outcast of heaven, and cursed amid my race.
Life will be terrible, but still 'tis life.
Life, life! ah! only life, with every ill!"
And from the forehead dark the red hand dash'd
The gathering drops of anguish and despair,
Leaving instead the crimson stains of guilt,
That grew and deepen'd as the answer came:—
"Go, murderer, forth: Omnipotence alone
Shall call thee when thy time to die is come,
And human power shall ne'er control thine end:
Therefore, henceforward bear this sacred stamp,
A mark to shield thee from the shafts of hate."
And, lo! upon his brow the gory stains
Were bright and hard, and shone a crown of gems,
And th' undried blood his hand had lately spill'd
Sparkled, a mass of rubies, in the sun.
And thus he lived apart from common fates,
Wearing defiantly his sign of shame,
Till mould conceal'd the symbol of his crime,
Wherein men seek for this unhallow'd gem,
Nor know, in groping for its costly light,
Whether or not they stir the dust of Cain.

EMERALDS.

When Eve came out of Eden, she still wore
Upon her grief-bow'd head a shining wreath,
Which Adam's hands had woven from the leaves

Of that fair tree whose fruit soon wrought their
doom.
But when the curse of God thrill'd earth's deep
heart,
The breath of His most solemn, mighty voice
Pass'd o'er that love-made crown, whose trembling
green
Grew petrified with awe to sparkling stone.
'Twas all of Eden that she bore away;
And yet, whene'er she bent her drooping brow
To Adam's breast, to slumber or to weep,
It hurt her like the memory of her sin,
And scarr'd her forehead's fairness with red frowns,
Till Adam seized it as a thing accursed,
And dash'd it into fragments mid the rocks.
The ancient Magi, skill'd in secret lore,
Knew well the value of its wondrous birth,
And bound the Emerald upon their hearts,
Engraven o'er with wisdom's mystic signs:
The talisman of knowledge gave them power.

MY PEARL.

Come talk with my lonely, sad soul to-night,
My Pearl from India's sea,
As white as the ocean's snowiest spray,
As round as its bright drops be.

Come tell me of wonderful things that live
In the wave's unmeasured blue,
Of all that is heaving and heaping there,
Far adown from mortal view.

Didst look from thy home in the tinted shell,
And watch the great monsters glide
With their monster-mates, stirring all the calm
Of the deeps beneath the tide?

Didst hear the mermaidens wooingly sing
To mermen from other waves?
Didst listen to love-stories even there,
In the hidden coral caves?

Hast thou seen the ruins of gallant ships
With gallant crews coming down,
While shrieks for life rang wild through the storm
Death's quiet alone could drown?

Hast thou seen the dead, in their mighty grave,
Astir mid the surging main,
As if the warm pulse of their living timo
Was filling their veins again,—

While fishes swam over each pallid face,
And sea-weed tangled their hair,
And the cold, blank eyes look'd evermore up
With stony and sightless stare?

But what canst thou know, pure child of the wave,
Of the breaking human hearts
That, still waiting, die in their distant homes
When the light of hope departs?

But most of all to my yearnings unfold
The unfathom'd mystery,
Ah, hast thou not learn'd it these many years?—
The great secret of the sea.

Has the ceaseless voice of the waters ne'er
Outspoken the marvellous pain
That upward wails from the innermost heart
Of the ever-restless main?

No; thou art silent, my beautiful Pearl,
Silent and white as the foam,
And canst utter no word of aught that dwells
In thy old, forgotten home.

Not the diver that brought thee out of the deep,
Nor thou, nor I, can e'er tell
The unlanguaged secret that strange, dark sea
For ages has guarded well.

A SOUND FROM THE BASTILLE.

"If, for my consolation, Monseigneur would grant me, for the sake of God and the Most Blessed Trinity, that I could have news of my dear wife, were it only her name on a card, to show that she is alive, it were the greatest consolation I could receive, and I would forever bless the greatness of Monseigneur."—Letter signed Louis Démery, dated "A la Bastille, 7me Oct., 1752."—("*Memoirs of the Bastille.*")

HEAR it! the voice of that poor prisoner's love
  Breaking all barriers of lone despair,
Of deep obscurity, rebellious pride,
  In yearning utterance of this touching prayer.
A human heart made meek by human pain,
  Suing to tyrant power,—but not for life,—
For more—for more, for one faint ray of hope,
  To calm suspense and end doubt's maddening strife.

There, in the silent darkness of his cell,
  Shut in from sunshine and the fair blue sky,
Day after day would memory's skill repaint,
  In richer dyes, life's precious things gone by;
The while those gray stone walls, cold, damp, and still,
  Mock'd every dream of passion and the past,
Till rage and grief and solitude of soul
  To burning tears forced manhood's strength at last.

Day after day he walk'd with her he loved,
  Touch'd her dear hand, look'd in her tender eyes,
Breathed her sweet name in dreams, and link'd it oft
  With soft, endearing words, and answer'd sighs,
Until his heart seem'd but to beat with hers
  Who gave to him each thought of her pure life,
And love o'erflow'd his spirit with a sense
  Of true religion, as he call'd her "wife."

And then to wake—to wake from blissful hours
  Of world-forgetting rapture, from a faith
In beauty, happiness, a home and heaven,
  To this dark dungeon and a living death!
To feel no more. no more, that darling head
  Nestling to his broad breast, and each white arm
Clinging to his proud strength, as there alone
  Her woman's weakness shrank from no alarm!

To rave 'gainst God and man,—to pray, to weep,
  To fancy jealous fears with fever'd brain,
To groan imploring cries for her dear life,
  Till dread of death became his keenest pain!
He could not die while she was yet alive;
  Yet, living, surely her great love could pierce
Through bolt and bar, o'er guard and moat and
    wall,
  And by some token end this conflict fierce.

These rulers of the land who kept him there,
  Accursed as they were, they still were men,—

Had hearts, souls, passions, feelings like his own,—
  Loved lovely women, and were loved again.
Perchance his voice, full of its yearning woe,
  Would strike a chord of pity in their breasts,
And, answering with one word, more joy would thrill
  His being than could sway their grandest guests.

And then he waited long,—till life and hope
  Died out together,—and to coming time
Left but this faded letter and a name,
  A broken heart's appeal to sceptred crime.
Those storied stones were witnesses of blood:
  A nation wept when impotent to save;
And earth responds to that poor captive's fate,
  That love is free in realms beyond the grave.

WORSHIP.

My God! my God! how thrills my mortal frame
  In tearful ecstasy of praise or prayer,
When, humbly lingering on the One Great Name,
  My soul, aspiring, finds its limit there.

And ofttimes, kneeling, in mine utmost need,
  With speechless awe my trembling spirit shrinks,
While bitterest cry of human pain or want
  In adoration's reverent silence sinks.

Yet, knowing Thee, the One forever true,
While earthly loves and earthly hopings end,
My heart in sorrow still sublimely yearns
Through all the universe to find its Friend.

And, childlike reaching to a Father's hand,
Unspoken thoughts creep upward to His throne;
And though I stood companionless mid men,
My God, Thou knowest I am ne'er alone.

EL DORADO.

'Twas autumn noon: beneath a lofty oak
I idly dream'd upon the hill-side green;
And all around morn's golden veil of light
Had shed a glory o'er the harvest-scene.

Below there spread a field of ripen'd corn,
Half reap'd, half waving in the passing breeze,
Waiting a couch within the empty wain
That stood with drowsy team 'neath neighboring trees.

The farmers, weary of their mid-day toil,
Had homeward turn'd their eager steps, to find
Some welcome rest around the groaning board,
Leaving their graceful sheaves, and me, behind

And farther off, like sparkling, jewell'd belt,
  The river shone, where stately ships went by,
Whose snowy sails, through clefts of verdure seen,
  By fleecy clouds seem'd mirror'd in the sky.

The balmy air just stirr'd the yellow grain,
  And, save the cattle's low, no sound arose,
But now and then an insect's droning chirp,
  To stir the silence of the day's repose.

And, floating downward through my leafy screen,
  A single ray like Jacob's ladder seem'd,
That upward reach'd to heavens of far-off years,
  Where phantoms of the past, like angels, gleam'd;

Hours that come no more, and hopes long gone,
  The memories of lost loves, and friendships dead,
Pale ghosts of passionate meetings and farewells,
  The shadows of old dreams, and tales oft read.

But most these last; for from my listless hand
  Had dropp'd the book my thoughts long linger'd
    o'er,
A stirring chronicle of times gone by,
  What men believed and did in days of yore.

Strange stories of the sea, and legends wild
  As this one by the ancient Arabs told,
Of Satan's hand outstretching from the wave
  To grasp the ship whose venture was too bold;

And those long-cherish'd fables of the West,
  The Golden City, and the Fount of Youth;
And all the list of brave, heroic men
  Who died in searching for their trusted truth;

Till mine own fancy, set aflame by dreams
  Of wonders hidden 'neath the Southern Cross,
In secret forests of that gorgeous land
  Stay'd not of life and hope to count the loss;

Saw only two brave Walters proudly sail
  From shores whose giant-queen bade each "God-
    speed,"
And "wore them in her heart," while, outward
    bound,
  Their fearless minds to danger gave no heed;

Forgetting all the while a foreign grave,
  Where Raleigh's son slept 'neath a tropic sky,—
Whose sire's last words were on a scaffold spoke,—
  "So hearts be right, what matter how heads lie?"

For all my thoughts were busy with the tale
  Of that old Spanish sailor who alone
Had walk'd through El Dorado's gilded streets,
  And seen the Inca on his ivory throne.

Till in my vision I arose, and pass'd
  Through opening ranks of plumed and bowing
    grain,

That like an army of raised dead closed up,
  With warning whisper that the quest was vain.

And at the river's edge I found a ship,
  That swiftly bore me over distant seas,
Until the water freshen'd 'neath the keel,
  The sails were wafted by a scented breeze;

And up a widening stream, upon whose shore
  Panthers and serpents, birds and lilies, drank,
As once in Eden by Euphrates' wave,
  Untamed, untrain'd, they shared the same green bank;

Until at last we anchor'd in a lake,
  Bearing an emerald island on its breast,
Whereon a marble structure stately rose,
  Whose open gate seem'd waiting for a guest.

In front a fount of liquid gold sprang up,
  In jewell'd basin sparkling still to fall,
And just beyond its porphyry columns rose,
  Strewn o'er with precious dust, the palace-hall.

Within, four gorgeous lamps burn'd day and night
  Before an altar, whereon dazzling shone
A burnish'd, golden sun, whose glowing rays
  Circled the Emperor on his ivory throne.

In silver robes, the people of the land
  Bow'd ever down before their hidden king,

And each received a priceless crown whose hand
  The tribute of a crystal heart could bring.

A stranger, 'wilder'd by the flashing light,
  I turn'd aside where other galleries led,
Where pictures hung whose colors were of gems,
  And topaz stars lit sapphire domes o'erhead.

Through piles of ingots and an India's wealth,
  Out in the sunshine roved my tireless feet,
Met marvels at each step, until at last
  I reach'd the entrance of the goldsmiths' street.

I cannot tell the lustre and the wealth
  That dazzled all my senses in one maze,
Till sudden blindness struck my wondering sight,
  In the swift flashing of a diamond's blaze.

And, stung with pain, I strain'd my smarting eyes,
  Still darken'd by the brightness of the stone,
Till from the fabled glories of a dream
  Came recognition of a scene well known.

The waving corn, the river winding past,
  The shining scythes, the empty, waiting wain,
And the great tree through whose thick-cluster'd leaves
  A noonday beam, straight darting, made my pain.

While pondering o'er the meaning of my dream,
  I raised the book, and on the open page

The rare, quaint author had his moral writ,
  Answering my thoughts in warning to his age:—

"Lost, lost, forever lost the old belief
  In golden quests that lured men o'er the seas.
Yet, readers dear, still keep an earnest faith
  In distant mysteries more rich than these.

"For still the eternal fount of life and youth
  Flows pure and fresh from out the great white throne,
And still the gilded city waits for guests,
  Whose streets are gold, whose walls are precious stone.

"And but one mortal—Christ's beloved John—
  Has seen this El Dorado's priceless state,
Wherein no sunlight but God's glory shines,
  And ever open stands each pearly gate.

"O weary wanderer through a desert world,
  See that the heart be crystal clear from sin
Thou layest before thy Sovereign's dazzling throne,
  That, crown'd with light, thy soul may dwell therein!"

THE DIFFERENCE.

In the parting glow of the summer sun,
I kiss'd her red lips ere the day was done,
  Clasping her close to my heart,—
Close to the heart that had loved her so well,
  Close to the heart that had loved her so long,
With such timid love it could only tell
  Its hope in another's song,—
Speaking a verse that floated through
  My memory as we watch'd the day
  'Twixt crimson portals fade away
Into the dark of dusky blue!
Her trembling hand fell away from my arm;
The blood flush'd her cheek like the wine that fills
  A transparent chalice of tinted pearl.
Madden'd by passion's unthinking alarm,
With my throbbing heart pulsing only thrills,
  Fevering hopes and fears, in a sudden whirl
          Of boldness and pain,
I seized her hand and look'd down in her eyes,
Dear eyes, that said more than only surprise,
Then hid their tears on my heaving breast.
          Ah! never again
Can life know moments so fleeting and blest!

In the parting glow of the winter sun,
I kiss'd her white lips ere the day was done,

Clasping her close to my heart,—
Close to the heart that was breaking with pain,
Close to the heart that grew gray with its woe,
Thinking that never! ah, never again
On earth I could hold her so,—
Thinking how soon the brown, damp mould
Would pillow the beautiful head,
And I alone, with my precious dead
Lying out in the bitter cold.
I murmur'd her name in passionate tones;
But the pure, closed lids hid her eyes' soft light,
And no blushes mantled the marble cheek.
The chamber of death echoed only groans,
That rang through the silent shadows of night,
Till dawn found me tearless, quiet, and weak
As a conquer'd child.
Then I kiss'd once more her pallid, still brow,
Ere they laid her beneath the falling snow,
And took up my burden of life again;
But mournful and wild
Ever sounds in my soul sad memory's strain!

THE TALK.

ATHALIE.—Oh, I am weary of this changeless round
Of dull monotony which men call life!
Existence should be more than merely breath,
And sleep, and caring for the outward sense.

The mind, the kernel of this mortal shell,
Was ne'er intended thus to wither up,
And, rotting, perish in its darken'd home;
Albeit 'tis true the nut must first be crush'd
Before the richness of the fruit is reach'd,
And often thus 'tis only suffering shows
The hidden ripeness of created souls.
But I would rather bear earth's fiercest pain
And walk amid the furnace of its wrath,
All scathed with wounds and sear'd with aching scars,
Treading with burning feet its fiery rage,
Than drag my being calmly, tamely out,
As I have seen at shows some conquer'd pard
Viewing with patience his confining cage,
As though he cared not for his fetter'd state,
Nor raged that each new hour would pass the same
The while the world was wide for his wild steps.
I hate such inert ease,—just feeling now
As if the pulses of my heart stood still,
Waiting for some great shock to send the blood
In leaping buoyancy through each glad vein.

EULALIE.—And yet, my friend, whene'er the heart's red stream
Too long and swiftly bounds in such fierce course,
The uncheck'd throbbing of its fever'd beats
Destroys the very life 'twas form'd to give.

ATHALIE.—I care not: death's still peace is better far

Than these mad aspirations of my soul,
This restless impotence of striving thought,
Impatient doubts, and unreach'd speechless hopes.
Thy calmer nature cannot comprehend
How all the daring of Crusading sires
Fires my lonely dreams with bitter scorn
Of woman's weakness, woman's dull content.
Oh! there are times when I could buckle on
Ancestral armor 'gainst a throng of foes,
And almost deem the world's arena small!

EULALIE.—Such field of action as your spirit seeks
Should never be a woman's battle-ground:
Her scene of warfare must be in her Home;
Her foes, the daily trials that harass
And fight against each struggling Christian's soul;
Her spotless shield, her purity and truth;
Her weapons, love and humble, holy faith;
Her armor, innocence; her leader, God;
Her fortress, prayer; her banner's sole device,
An open Bible with its well-worn leaves;
Her greatest conquests, her own passions tamed;
The highest captives by her triumphs won,
Her children's hearts, and husband's fond esteem;
Her proudest trophy, her own happy hearth;
And men will rise before her honor'd head,
"And call her bless'd," who strives and conquers thus.
Ah! I would rather be the placid star
That lights a good man's dwelling with its rays,

Than shine the brightest sun that ever shed
Its brilliant beams upon a dazzled world.

ATHALIE.—And such should be your destiny, dear
friend.
Earth's sweetest flowers ever seek the shade;
The fragrant violet hides its lowly head
Within the waving grass, just peeping up
To catch, 'twixt dewy blades, a glimpse of heaven!
But the glorious Rose, the garden queen,
Sits proudly on its throne of green, and wears
Its sparkling coronet of cloud-born gems.
Only the King of Night and Song dare woo
The Sovereign of the Flowers; and minstrel strains
Have ever told how vain his plaintive notes
Whose sweetness wins the adoration mute
Of every blossom save the one he sues.

EULALIE.—And so the rose drops lonely from her
stalk,
Because she sighs for Zephyr: 'tis for him
To win the passing fancy of a god,
She scorns the bliss of kindred sympathy,
And turns aside from true and earnest love.
A woman's ideal's not a woman's fate!

ATHALIE.—Hush! you are all too cold for dreams,
while life
For me is woven through with fancy's threads.
Ah! years ago the angels came from heaven

And lost their Paradise for woman's smile;
But now they come no more. Is it because
There is no being pure and high enough
Now in this world to win a spirit's love?
The sons of men are all too gross and low
To seek a soul! they but the casket woo.
Eye worships eye, and sense adores the flesh!
The jewel is not sought: perchance, if found,
The value is unknown, and it drops back
Into the olden darkness whence it shone,
And hides once more its brightness in the dust!
Spirit alone should e'er a spirit win;
And those high natures that could fearless share
A god's or angel's love were worthy, sure,
To claim the homage that immortals yield.
Do angels fold their wings no more on earth?
And, Eulalie, all lovely as thou art,
Methinks that thou shouldst gain a spirit's love,
E'en though he left an Eden for the prize!

EULALIE.—Oh! 'tis such dreams as these, dear Athalie,
That make thy heart like to the great, sad sea,
Forever moaning with a wild unrest
For Dian's unattainable, far shore.
Hast seen it upward heave its quivering waves,
Like hoping lover stretching out his arms,
To catch his mistress to his panting breast?
Who sees them feebly fall with mocking gaze,
Knowing the witchery of her next bright smile
Will raise and swell the ebbing tide of hope!

Thus ever yearning for an unreach'd goal,
Thy restless soul-depths murmur with despair
Or sing with joy. True Happiness stands oft
Beside our very threshold, yet we spring
With eager footstep to pursue some shape,
Some visionary phantom that holds forth
The tempting semblance of alluring fruit,
Which when we strive to reach, we find but shades,
That ever fly, yet still excite desire,
While the real good we might have won at first
Has vanish'd in the turnings of our race.

ATHALIE.—Our happiness lies only in ourselves,
And how and where our inner selves expand.
And in the ocean's fathomless abyss
Are cavern'd mysteries and wonderous rare things;
Bright heaps of priceless gems there hoarded up
Are gather'd by the foam of outer waves.
The sea is but the earth's great, throbbing heart,
Still rich in jewels, though the moon is far,
And pearls and rubies sleep within its depths,
Like lovely dreams in unroused human minds.
Yet as the vast Leviathan disturbs
The water's deep repose, so comes the hour
Of inspiration to the thinking brain,
Which, laboring with the burden that it bears,
Pants with a feverish pain till tuneful words,
Like breezes music-laden from the land,
Bring quick relief by lulling to repose
The writhings of the sudden waken'd power,

And from its secret caves each storm's strong hand
Casts out its jewels on the world's wide shore,
To sparkle there.

EULALIE.— Or else, perchance, to lie,
Trampled by careless feet, in graves of sand.
Thou readest thus a lesson from the sea,
Yet thou, with all thy yearnings and wild dreams,
Art voiceless to thy race, and cast no gems
Up from the treasury of thy real soul.
The truest song springs from the deepest thought;
And wouldst thou shake the sloth of visions off,
And chain their beauty unto kindred words,
The echoing Earth would bear thee in its arms,
A crown'd Corinna, mid its proudest fanes.
This is thy want, my friend,—the will to work,
Instead of waiting for a chance reward.
Ambition, Genius, like hidden fires,
Consume thine hours, whose upward-mounting flame
Is quench'd in idle tears of timid pride!

ATHALIE.—'Tis true! 'tis true! How, Eulalie, didst thou
So read the passions of my lonely moods?
I will be up and doing, as thou sayest,
Nor longer in mere dreams thus waste my youth.
My precious gift of song, the breath divine
With which God waked my soul to higher life,
Henceforth I hold thee as a heavenly trust,
A stainless flower, to be guarded pure

From taint of worldly touch, the while it throws
Its wealth of odor upon every breeze.
Farewell! farewell! I thank thee that thy words
Have set the goal for which my spirit longs.
And now, whate'er may be my coming fate,
This thought of me shall still be thine, my friend:
Thou'st starr'd my solitude with one great hope!
Farewell! farewell!

EULALIE.— Oh, Athalie!
She's gone! she's gone! I had not meant to rouse
Such energy of daring in her soul!
And yet, perchance, 'tis well: the might is there,
And needed but a spur to show its strength.
'Tis strange that thus a summer evening's talk
Should grow from idle fancies to such end,
That one should read the purpose of her life
And forward spring to grasp a waiting crown,
While I—well, I will wait in patience here,
Till fate shall seek me in my quiet home,
Wherein, some day, perchance yon noble soul,
World-wearied by the very fame it seeks,
Will find a refuge from the praise of men,
And, coming back to youth's first friendly trust,
Say, "Eulalie, since long ago we talk'd
One eve together on this velvet knoll,
My life has learn'd this lesson from my thoughts:
That howsoe'er on earth we frame our hopes,
Whatever paths we tread, at last we know
No destiny is finish'd in this world!"

THE TOMB IN AVENTICUM.

When the night was dark and dreary, and I sat alone
to read
Of many a martial history, many a gallant deed,

Then, amid the noise of battles, the strife of warriors bold,
Came the echoes of a story from the perish'd days
of old.

As the notes of gentler music stealing mid a warlike
strain,
All my feverish dreams of glory it restored to peace
again.

In an ancient, ruin'd city, where the ivy clothes the
wall,
Where the broken columns moulder, and the dust
is like a pall;

Where the tottering arches tremble in the breeze
that passes by,
And where palaces and temples in dark, scatter'd
masses lie;

Where, in roads where conquerors triumph'd, only
stones and silence sway,
And where all that marks the Present is a shrine
where pilgrims pray;

Here they found who seek in ruins an inscription uneffaced,
Touching record of dead ages, by forgotten workmen traced;

Tomb of Julia Alpinula, with her epitaph and fate,
The patriot's virgin daughter, victims both of Roman hate;

Telling of a fearful struggle, of Helvetian valor vain,
Of the legions shouting "Victory!" o'er the red couch of the slain;

Of the city's humble message of submission and despair,
Despatch'd by reverent fathers with staffs and snowy hair;

Of the foeman's haughty answer, his unbending, stern decree,
That the idol of the nation, rebellion's price must be.

This, with aged eyes o'erflowing, in trembling, broken tones,
Told the sages in their council, mid a storm of sighs and groans.

But the people—crush'd, dishonor'd, by the fetter of defeat—
Walked, wrapp'd in sullen silence, through each noise-deserted street.

None had dared to curse the tyrant, none had sought
his guarded tent,
To plead the cause of innocence, of a life in virtue
spent.

But the doom'd one had a daughter, a pure priest-
ess young and fair,—
All her woman's timid nature render'd bold by fierce
despair.

Through the warriors' encampment, through the
mocking soldier-host,
With filial speed she hasten'd, like a white-robed,
fleeting ghost,

Till before the Roman general, with panting grace,
she kneel'd,
Like a snow-flake from the heavens on that dark,
ensanguined field.

There, with prayers like inspiration, she implored
her parent's life,
Kiss'd the conqueror's bloody hand, weapon-hard-
en'd in the strife,

Invoked in supplication the dear phantoms of his
dead,
Begg'd, for sake of living blessings, mercy's gene-
rous balm to shed,

All the while still looking upward with her tearful,
earnest eyes,
And her quivering lips low murmuring all her
heart's entreating cries;

Till the leaders who were fathers, standing in the
general's tent,
Felt their anger melt to softness, and kind looks of
pity lent.

But she plead to sterner metal than his iron-hilted
sword;
For he cast aside the weeper, and gave the fatal
word!

She clung to him like ivy, never loosen'd once her
hold,
Promised all that life could offer,—hidden stores of
secret gold,

Swore to pledge her whole existence as his hum-
blest, lowest slave,
To redeem this well-beloved one from the shadow
of the grave.

Once again he dash'd her from him, coldly bade the
herald fly
To proclaim that, ere the sun set, her rebellious sire
should die!

Then arose with haughty calmness the patriot's
only child,
Her slight form rearing proudly, hushing all her
anguish wild.

And amid those arméd warriors a sudden shiver
swept,
To see such lightning flashing from the eyes so
lately wept.

Then, clear as silver tocsin in a god's most holy shrine,
Rang her tones throughout the silence, like an oracle
divine,

As she call'd with solemn vengeance a great curse
from mighty Jove
On his household, on his kindred, upon all that he
should love.

Child, woman, priestess, prophetess, they quail'd
before the spell,
All their stubborn natures shuddering as the fearful
accents fell.

Then forth, like holy thing, unharm'd, with proud
mien and tearless eye,
Went to meet her martyr'd father, on his bloody
bier to die.

Fifteen hundred years had vanish'd, when, amid
the ruin'd state
Of Aventicum's dead glory, men read her noble fate.

Who there cared to know what monarch had trod
those stately halls,
Where now an echoing footstep breaks a quiet that
appalls?

Who ask'd what chariots triumph'd, what name
was rallying word,
What shouts those walls had startled, what prayers
those altars heard?

For 'tis not to these the stranger, when fresh from
history's page,
Turns, searching for the beauties of a buried, distant age;

But, apart from meaner relics, seeks the sepulchres
of yore,
Till the urns where heroes moulder all the perish'd
Past restore.

Tomb of Julia Alpinula, what mute eloquence is
thine,
Filling all our hearts with fragrance like the incense from a shrine!

And our thoughts grow rich with rapture, recollecting thy brave deed,
And we yearn across life's ruins with a newer, purer
need,—

Need to find amid its temples, mid its castles overthrown,
More of love's rare aloe-flowers, in the ages blooming
lone.

THE QUESTION OF THE DAY IN 1860.

Dissolve the Union, that the worn-out thrones
Across the sea may mock us as we fall,
And envious powers grow secure in ill,
And crush their peoples with an iron heel
To grind out gold and blood from subject-worms,
That they no more, uplooking from the dust,
May westward turn with hearts of yearning faith,
And murmur to their children, "Ah, 'tis there!
The land of promise, wherein men may think,
And not be slain for speech or robb'd of right!"

Dissolve this Union, and dear hope dies out
In all the eager souls that watch its stars
Rise steadfast o'er the earth with growing light.
Pray that they prove not meteors that fade,
When they should guide all steerless ships of state
To one great haven of ensampled peace.
Save our great eagle and her eyrie broad
From pecking crows, and vultures that await
Her parting struggles to usurp her nest,
Lest e'en the pure, white stripe of our proud flag
Be dipp'd by anarchy's foul hand in gore,
And wave no more the beacon of the world.

See how she sits, our young and lovely land,
Throned on two seas that crouch beside her state,
Queen mid the nations, lifting her fair brow,

Serene with prosperous peace and plenty's smile,
Crown'd but with beauty o'er the heads of kings.
Shall we, her children, borne upon her breast,
Thus make her tremble with the awful dread
Lest we, her own, shall tear her limb from limb,
And shroud in mourning all the brilliant hopes
That wait upon her glory, while her knell
Shall be old Tyranny's glad, scornful laugh?

In her deep heart she holds some mighty dead,
Who stirr'd the nations with their words, and bore
With Atlas strength a world of care and thought.
Alas that they, the giants of those days,
Awake not now to hurl upon her foes
The curse of God on parricidal sin,
And win with charméd eloquence of yore
The sluggish masses to a holy rage,
Would crush the serpents that now hiss and sting,
Crawling in highest places of the land!

Up, people of the States that love your homes!
Up, gallant hearts that throb with pure disdain
Of traitorous arts! Up, slumbering souls of fire!
Build ye a Haman's gallows for these knaves
That dare to raise a voice or hand to break
The sweet relationship our fathers left
To bind us all, cemented with their lives!
O North and South,—two brothers of one birth,—
Meet ye again as they at Peniel met,
Jacob and Esau, thinking each of strife,

Yet, when they came anear, wept with pure love
Upon each other's neck; that both may say,
"Keep that thou hast, for God has dealt
Most graciously with each; and thus we see
Each other's face, as 'twere the face of God,
Shining with blessing; and the Lord of Hosts
Watch between thee and me for evermore!"

THE HESPERIDES.

"The Hesperides," or "The Western Maidens," were three celebrated nymphs. They are said to have been the daughters of Night, and to have had no father. Their home was beyond the bright ocean. When the bridal of Jupiter and Juno took place, all the deities came, bearing nuptial presents for the bride; among them came the goddess of Earth, bringing with her branches having golden apples growing thereon. Juno, being greatly pleased with the branches of golden fruit, begged of Earth to plant them in her gardens, which extended as far as Mount Atlas. The request was granted, and the Hesperides were set to guard them. But, alas! the fruit was too tempting; and, like our first mother, they put forth their hands and plucked for themselves. Juno was so enraged at this conduct, that she sent a great dragon to guard the precious fruit. Hercules was sent by Eurystheus to bring some of it. On his quest he came to the river Eridanus, and inquired of some nymphs where the apples were to be obtained. They directed him to Nereus, whom he found asleep: him he bound and held fast till he told him. He visited Egypt, roamed through Arabia, over the mountains of Libya; he then reached the eastern course of the ocean, which he crossed in the cup of the sun-god. He now came to where Prometheus lay chained with a bird feeding on his liver; he shot the bird and delivered Prometheus, who, out of gratitude, warned him not to go himself after the apples, but to send Atlas, and in the mean time support the heavens in his stead. Atlas, accordingly, went for the apples, and, when he returned, proposed to carry them to Eurystheus himself. This Prometheus seemingly acceded to, but asked him to take hold of the heavens while he put a pad on the head of his friend Hercules. The unwary Atlas threw down the apples and resumed his burden, when Hercules snatched up the fruit and went on his way.

We seek it in our glowing youth,—
That wondrous garden far away;
We deem its golden fruit still waits
For us alone each passing day.
We close our eyes to see them shine,
We wake to strain our utmost speed,
Forgetful of the dragon-guard,
The tempting branch our sorest need!

We cross the changing foam of life,
Nor pause to measure depths below:
The sun-god's radiant cup upbears
Our hot hearts o'er the wave's dark flow.
We scale the mountains, pass the waste,
Yet linger, mid the earnest quest,
By murmuring streams, 'neath harvest-moons,
Of siren nymphs the willing guest!

We free the chain'd Promethean thought
  From tyrant Custom's gnawing beak;
Yet, strong in faith, the heavens rest
  Upon the dreams we never speak.
The years grow gray; unwither'd still
  The golden apples sparkle there;
We know some path must reach the gates,
  Mount Atlas bounds our worst despair!

Alas, alas for all our hopes!
  Our heart-beats fainter throb at last;
We droop our heads on Memory's breast,
  Hesperides was in the Past!
We think again of harvest-moons,
  The dead we knew, the kisses sweet:
The high endeavor leaves our soul;
  We only long the loved to meet;
Once more the passionate old thrill
  Of yearning to our lives is given;
God, Death, and Truth alone reveal
  The real Hesperides is heaven!

AFTER THE TRIUMPH.

I, Zenobia, queen of the wide East,
Even I have swell'd a Roman monarch's march
Of triumph through his Rome! I, that did wear
Imperial purple in mine own far land,

Dragg'd royal robes in mockery through the dust,
Sweeping the way before Aurelian's car,
My conqueror's herald, who then smiled to see
His worthiest foe, a woman and unqueen'd,
Thus stared at by the common crowd, whose shouts
Would hail his victor with as loud acclaim.
Gods! how they sneer'd because I rear'd my head,
Drooping with jewels, regally as he,
Whilst German amazons wept tears of shame!
I, that did come of kingly loins, and bore
Three princes to their crowned sire, thus walk'd,
Endiadem'd, the sceptred peasant's slave!
I, that had awed Armenia, and sway'd
The restless Arabs with my white, strong hand,
That allied with the Persian, and have chain'd
My own ancestral Egypt to my throne,—
I bear these fetters; golden though they be,
They bind my flesh like tighten'd coils of snakes,
And crush my heart beneath their splendid weight.
O Tadmor of the desert! isle of palms!
Zenobia lost herself in losing thee,
And thou art lost in her that had the will
To make thee rival this proud western state!
Soon shalt thou hide the glories of my reign,
Thy gorgeous beauty, and thy gather'd wealth,
Beneath entombing sands; no sovereign more
Shall raise thee to the height from which I fell!
Oh, why was I so form'd that clear disdain
Of female arts destroy'd my power to win?
Swart Cleopatra with her eyes and lips

Conquer'd her conqueror, kept her royal name,
And ruled the serf she purchased with a kiss!
I too, perchance, if I had deign'd to sue,
To smile, and deck myself with tender wiles,
Might thus have gain'd fame's immortality,
Mistress of the world's one master, whom this Rome
Will make a god and leave me mortal still!
For I do know that I am beautiful,
And, like dead Antony, Aurelian too
Is but a man! But I went forth to meet
My enemy the emperor like a king,
Or, as in other times I rode beside
My noble husband, girded with my sword,
To strike swift terror through the great king's realm.
I headed mine own troops,—forgot to be
A woman, till I should have thought alone
How it became a vanquish'd queen to die.
I loathe myself that I did dare to live,
The Roman scoff, to fill a Roman's pride,
Whilst my Palmyra shone beneath the sun,
Dreading no slaughter in the open field,
Yet trembling mid rude soldiers of the camp
To face a captive's grim and unchaste death,
Leaving my name to future ages' scorn,
Whose history shall record, on living page,
That in their hours of like and worst despair
Great Cleopatra died, Zenobia lived!

THE POET'S WIFE.

He was so high above the common herd,
And I so far below his lofty state,
How could I deem that he should lift me up
To share his fate?

He pass'd so many eager watchers by,
Scorn'd wealth and mighty royalties of grace,
To draw me from the dust, and give to me
The wifely place!

I could have stay'd forever at his feet,
Unnoticed, learning snatches of his song,
That stirr'd the world's deep heart, and made sad souls
For action strong!

I did not seek to come into his life:
The wide earth worshipp'd him, and so might I.
'Twas happiness to stand apart and see
His face go by!

But when he took me in his folding arms,
And look'd in mine with loving, mournful eyes,
And laid my head upon his human heart,
My soul's surprise

So kept me silent that I dared not ask
  Why he from queendoms thus had turn'd away,
His laurel crown upon my humble brow
    Proudly to lay.

There only thrill'd through my unspoken bliss
  Remember'd words that long ago were sung,
Our bridal omen :—"Whom immortal gods
    Do love, die young!"

I stand beside him in his victor's car,
  I hear the shouts for every triumph won,
And mark his quiet smile at such reward
    For labor done,

And know he looks across the present years
  To coming ages that shall keep his fame,
While men shall know me chiefly as the one
    That bore his name.

I minister unto his daily wants;
  I hold his tired head upon my breast;
I smooth aside all petty things that mar
    His perfect rest.

But this is all! I cannot comprehend
  The wondrous thoughts that make his pale cheeks
    glow,
The new-born dreams that in his teeming brain
    To giants grow.

I cannot soar with him through rapturous flights,
Nor share his inspiration's trembling hour,
Nor grasp the beautiful with throbbing pulse
Of conscious power.

He never seems to marvel that I move
Mid household duties as if my sole care
Was woman's thrift, and every night to raise
My voice in prayer.

He knows not that I feel aught save content,
Sitting among the violets alone,
Outside the Eden where God's angels talk
Around his throne.

Yet something in my quiet nature calms
The fever of his ever-yearning life;
And so I hide the secret of my pain,—
My inward strife.

Ah, well! I shall die soon, and then—and then—
In heavens of progress I, perhaps, may grow
To his mind's stature,—his own truer wife
Than here below!

That there at last, half strangers through this life,
Our unveil'd souls may evermore respond,
And seal, in mansions of Our Father's house,
Our marriage bond.

Only God love him when my love shall pass
  Out of his earthly home, and teach him still,
Amid his high aspirings, to bow down
      To God's good will!

It is his poet's fate that he must be
  Within the world with his great soul alone,
And only meet upon Death's mystic shore
      His very own.

1861.

THE SOVEREIGN OF THE PAMPAS.

Morning on the lone and silent Pampas,
Those dewless plains of long and stirless grass
O'erarch'd by skies unshadow'd by a cloud,
And all unbroken in their sea-like calm,
Except where, here and there, a parching palm
Uprears its barren stem, and marks to sight
Some space between the mingling earth and heaven,
Or musky odors of the arid ground
Thicken the air, amid whose torrid heat
Rise vapory columns like the smoke of fires!
Solemn and still those vast savannas reach
Through level solitudes of countless miles,
Unsought by man, and whose untrodden depths
No taint, perchance, have borne of human death!
And thus they seem'd upon this fervid morn,
When the hot sun, like a great flaming eye,

Saw motion mid those withering waves of green,
That onward swell'd from the horizon's verge,
And stirr'd to life a myriad hidden things,
That fluttering swarm'd from midst the sheltering
blades
Before th' advancing dust that broke their rest,
As, panting, snorting in their thirsty haste,
A troop of desert horses rush'd along,
Trampling the crackling verdure in their race,
Startling the brooding silence of the waste
With insect voices and their own wild tones.
On, on they dash, creating with their speed
And noisy breaths the movement of a wind,
And raining foam on long unwater'd soil.
They pause; they wheel; they circle in a group,—
Impatient paw the ground,—take counsel short,—
Break,—toss their flowing manes,—and start again,
In compact throng, towards their unreach'd goal,
Still straining blood-shot eyes in search of streams,
And following one that ever leads the way,
Chief of the horde in speed, in grace, in choice,—
A chestnut mare, with stately, curving neck,
And small proud head, that on the forehead bore
A snowy star, as though to mark command,
Whose tapering limbs had borne her in the van,
With silky hair and shining coat unfleck'd.

No nomad kept the record of her kin,—
A prouder wealth than his own straight descent
From Ishmael sire: yet every step and turn

Betray'd an Arab ancestry of race,—
Some noted dam by Spanish conquerors won
In Moorish raid, and brought across the sea
To lose a master in some Indian fight
And find wild freedom in those Western wilds!
No Adam her untutor'd gambols check'd,
And no alluring Eve, with timid hand,
Tempted that arching neck to curbing rein;
No whisper'd spell could quell her flash of rage;
No spur or lash had goaded her quick blood.
She knew not man: her will or wants alone
Had led her where she would, controll'd the herd,
And, where no human reason sway'd the sense,
Her untaught instinct soar'd almost to thought.

Her home was all the Pampas, and her course
Unbounded save by rivers, on whose shores
A thousand colors blended in one mass,
And song and odor fill'd the forest-shade;
And thitherward she guided now the troop,
Till in the burning noon they cease their speed,
To rest recumbent mid the fading grass.

They sleep; while she, less wearied, stands on watch,
And casts upon her comrades now and then,
That only stir beneath an insect's sting,
A glance of mingled pity and contempt,
That softens into almost human love.
Sudden she lifts her drooping head, and looks

With eager gaze across the changeless scene,
As though to her keen sense some sight or sound
Gave thrilling warning that she dared not slight,—
Some token of near water, some faint breeze,
So faint it scarcely bent the slightest herb,—
Some breath of perfumed freshness from afar,
Mingling with hers, and dying as it came.
She starts; sho moves; she stops to look again
Upon her tired mates, as though in doubt
To stir them to uncertain search once more,
Or seek herself all peril and reward,
Then bear, with frame refresh'd, the tidings back,
And with unerring knowledge lead them on.
She turns; she waits; another scented breeze
Just lifts the wavy length of her dark mane;
She snuffs the passing gale with nostril wide,
She beats with restless limbs the scorching ground,
Gives the loud signal that awakes the rest,
Then forward bounds, and onward, onward flies.

And now they leave behind the sterile waste,
The shorter grasses break not 'neath their tread,
And here and there a tree gives welcome shade;
Now groups of palms, now thicker copses, rise,
And now entangled arches hidden bear
Unnumber'd choristers in leafy homes;
Now falls the volador's ripe, winged fruit,
And now the gaumo's silvery stamens shine;
The Saint-Esprits hang snowy in the air,
And soon in various and vivid hues

The clustering blossoms cover roots and trunks;
While in the darkening woods a myriad plumes
Dash changing rainbows through each open space;
They wind through all,—now leaping some old tree
Dragg'd down to earth by weight of twining vines,
Now through some path first widen'd by their
course,
Treading out freshness with each fleeting foot;
And now their chests part back the trembling ferns,
Uprousing slumbering serpents with their steps;
And more than once their stiffen'd ears upstart
At sight of glaring eyes in shadow'd lairs.
Now, now the trees grow fewer, and there swells
The welcome melody of water's sound;
Yet, struggling on mid sweeping branches still,
They see the sparkling beach, and cool, wet sand;
Then from the forest spring o'er jaguar dead,
And lave their swollen tongues in waves of life,
Whose distant falls make music mid the mist!

Sudden all gambols cease. The shrinking group
Together press, with looks of mortal fear,
As one shrill cry of anguish cleaves the air
And scares to silence all the woodland tribes.
And then a muffled sound of cracking bones
Proclaims the monster coils that quickly make
Of grace and beauty but a shapeless mass.
There, quivering, lay their wild, free, stately chief,
Clasp'd in a mighty boa's dread embrace,
That, from the nearest tree swift darting, caught

The richest prize to gorge his tempted watch!
Across the glossy neck the black, cold head
Droop'd, that the slimy tongue might reach the breast,
While each entwining fold, more tightly wound,
Crush'd out the ebbing life in shortening breaths.
Her comrades fly, back through the forest-aisles,
Back to their prairie home, and leave her there
With that great serpent, terror, and her death.
But when the Southern Cross began to bend,
And moonlight mingled all the hues of earth
In one soft radiance of silver sheen,
Still mid the placid quiet of the night
The sated monster stretch'd his torpid length,
Beside the mangled victim of his power,
Who, e'en too large for his elastic throat,
Was left for that dead jaguar she had spurn'd.
A noise disturbs the feasted monster's sleep;
But, ere the languid reptile rears its head,
Unnumber'd vengeful hoofs, with eager rage,
Stamp out the life and break the striving coil;
And when the condors gather'd in the morn,
One fatal foe across the other lay!

CHATTERTON.

The boy came up to London, high in heart
And beautiful in face,—a dreamer born,
With genius for a soul; earnest hope
Wing'd his wild thoughts of fame, and lonely pride
Saw with clear eyes the lowness of the race
That young ambition long'd to mould and rule.
The great town lay before him: from that mass
Of throbbing life his able hand would snatch
Cool laurel leaves, fresh with the dew of praise,
To crown his fever'd and work-wearied brain.
Within himself he felt expanding germs
Of unshaped visions swelling into song,
And heard the echoes ringing through the world
Down all the ages, till the tones sublime
Met the last trumpet's sound, and mingled then
With music of Eternity's long hymn!
His spirit leap'd to greet the coming minds
Should stand apart from all the meaner herd,
Monarchs by right divine, whose grand words
Would hail him worthy to wear royal robes
And walk with them in amaranthine fields.
The sense of power thrill'd the slender frame,
Fired the soft eye, dash'd from th' aspiring heart
All stings of memory, poverty's sharp chill,
Vague yearnings for the unattain'd, and e'en
The wild unrest that urged his onward steps
From home and kindred towards an unknown fate.

The world was wide before him; he was strong
To wrestle till he placed his conquering foot
Upon its neck to reach his victor's car;
And then—and then—why, let the dim Then come!

The boy came up to London. Day by day
The coils of destiny tighten'd round his life,
As hard reality stripp'd off all veil,
And hour by hour the hot, exultant glow
Of passionate, eager hope died from his dreams.
The goal receded, and grim, sickening want
Mock'd his white lips at every hungry moan!
The great gift-pearl, crown-jewel for a world,
Was trod by sightless swine in misery's mire!
The golden grain of lofty thought was ground,
Like common grist, in mills of sneers and sale,
And eat by hinds that never cared to know
What laden sheaf had borne such wondrous bread!
And on the street the busy, selfish crowd
Moved to and fro, nor deem'd that midst them stood
One greater than themselves: so well the gods
Wear mortal shapes when banish'd from their right!
And if mid waiting weeks came up a voice
Of recognition from the throng that hail'd
An unknown mind, he only smiled to see
Those bearded men by boyhood so befool'd,
And work'd a lower vein than this that won
The wine of praise, but not one taste of meat!
Until at last, uprising from his toil,
Madden'd by living, fetter'd by coarse needs,

He look'd once more into the night, earth's night,
And at the distant stars, glittering and cold
And pitiless, and, with his burning eyes
Searching the darkness, bade farewell to hope,
Drain'd hemlock, and lay prayerless down to sleep.

The boy came up to London,—and died young!
The days wore on, and still the sun shone bright;
The people came and went, and smiled and wept,
And all the outward show of life changed naught,
Though he was not! Great Nature gives no sign
When human creatures drop pain's heavy cross,
To rest within her breast; Greece never shook
Because Apollo soar'd from her dull plain,
To share divine ambrosia at the feasts
Amid Olympus' mists! Only long years,
Slow-sweeping into ages, taught at last
To reverent hearts what greatness there died young,
And how, perhaps, out of that fever'd youth
And restless scorn a something might have come,
When mellowing time had ripen'd reason's growth,
Could sway the listening ages into awe,
And give to England one more mighty name,
To lift her royalty its own height higher!

Died young! And when, one morn, they found him
thus,
The war of passion still on that white face,
The fragments of his work about him strewn,
The poison at his side, and over all

The arching sky, was there no lesson writ
In that short life, that sad, unhappy death,
Of warning unto men, that such as he
Are sent unto the earth, as oft of old
God's messengers within His city cried,
Whose people stoned them?—and so One did weep
To utter o'er the place, "Woe! woe! O thou
That slayest the prophets that are sent to thee!"
1862.

TIME AND THE SEA.

Up from his mighty deeps old Ocean roll'd,
To the majestic music of his waves,
That swell'd towards the sunlight and soft air,
Above unnumber'd wrecks and human graves.
Upon the shell-strewn shore the steps of Time
Scarce left their trace, as, counting one by one
The billows and the minutes as they came,
He sigh'd to see his sand so swiftly run;

Till suddenly the murmur of the sea
Grew to the language that all Nature knows,
And broke at last upon his listening sense,
That caught new meanings in its ebbs and flows:—
"Strong as thou art in thy destroying power,
To me alone thy shape no terror brings:
Thy mowing scythe no impress e'er can leave
Upon my closing foam or secret springs!

"Man fears alike my depths and thy sure dart;
Within my hidden caves, as on thy path,
The ruins of his loftiest works are strewn,
Himself the noblest wreck that feeds our wrath!
And he, the last created, sovereign mind,
Trembles to tread in our recorded track,—
To trust his dear ones to our treacherous care;
For Time and Ocean yield no treasures back!

"Thou shakest kingdoms into desert dust,
And leadest nations, blinded, to their fall;
Life's grandest, loveliest, mightiest things
Own that thy mouldering touch is on them all!
But only I in the wide, changing world,
Thine equal from the first, unalter'd still,
Sweep through thy realms, nor show one mark of thine,
Whilst thou thyself art gray with gather'd ill!

"Pass on, O Time! Ocean, alone thy peer,
Can laugh to scorn or wrestle with thy hand;
For Earth is ours, its mysteries and hopes,—
Mine the vast deep, and thine the crumbling land!"
Time turn'd his glass, and answer'd, as he moved
Beside the limit of the water's space,
Just casting, as he spoke, into their tide
A little stone, that sank and left no trace:

"Thus thou and I shall sink, O boasting waves,
Into eternity, on that great day

When o'er the land and sea the angel's voice
  Proclaims that thou and I shall pass away.
Both servants of one Master, each must work
  Appointed ways towards the destined end,
And when His will, 'who doeth all things well,'
  Is fully wrought, to our dead past descend!
Whilst man, whom here we hold within our grasp,
  Forever lives; for life is God's own breath,
The soul, that with the heavenly host and Him
  Shall watch the close of Time, and Ocean's death!"

AFTER THE BATTLE.

Hold the lantern aside, and shudder not so!
There's more blood to see than this stain on the
    snow!
There are pools of it, lakes of it, just over there,
And fix'd faces all streak'd, and crimson-soak'd hair!
Did you think, when we came, you and I, out to-
    night
To search for our dead, yon would be a fair sight?

You're his wife; you love him,—you think so; and I
Am only his mother: my boy shall not lie
In a ditch with the rest, while my arms can bear
His form to a grave that mine own may soon share!
So, if your strength fails, best go sit by the hearth,
While his mother alone seeks his bed on the earth.

You will go! then no faintings! Give me the light,
And follow my footsteps!—*my* heart will lead right!—
Ah, God! what is here? a great heap of the slain,
All mangled and gory!—What horrible pain
These beings have died in! Dear mothers, ye weep,
Ye weep, oh, ye weep o'er this terrible sleep!

More! more! Ah! I thought I could nevermore
know
Grief, horror, or pity for aught here below,
Since I stood in the porch and heard his chief tell
How brave was my son, how he gallantly fell!
Did they think I cared then to see officers stand
Before my great sorrow, each hat in each hand?

Why, girl, do you feel neither reverence nor fright,
That your red hands turn over towards this dim
light
These dead men that stare so? Ah, if you had kept
Your senses this morning ere his comrades had left,
You had heard that his place was worst of them all—
Not mid the stragglers—where he fought he would
fall!

There's the moon through the clouds: Christ, Christ,
what a scene!
Dost thou from thy heavens o'er such visions lean
And still call this curst world a footstool of thine?
Hark! a groan; there, another,—here in this line
Piled close on each other.—Ah, here is the flag,
Torn, dripping with gore—Pah! they died for this rag!

Here's the voice that we seek.—Poor soul, do not
start:
We're women, not ghosts.—What a gash o'er the
heart!
Is there aught we can do? a message to give
To any beloved one? I swear, if I live,
To take it for sake of the words my boy said,
"Home," "mother," "wife"—ere he reel'd down
'mong the dead!

But, first, can you tell where his regiment stood?
Speak, speak, man, or point!—'twas the Ninth!—
Oh, the blood
Is choking his voice!—what a look of despair!
There, lean on my knee, while I put back the hair
From eyes so fast glazing—Oh, my darling, my own,
My hands were both idle when you died alone!

He's dying—he's dead!—close his lids—let us go.
God's peace on his soul!—If we only could know
Where our own dear one lies!—My soul has turn'd
sick!
Must we crawl o'er these bodies strewn here so
thick?
I cannot! I cannot! How eager you are!
One might think you were nursed on the red lap of
War.

He's not here,—and not here!—What wild hopes
flash through
My thoughts, as foot-deep I stand in this dread dew

And cast up a prayer to the blue, quiet sky!—
Was it you, girl, that shriek'd? Ah! what face doth
lie
Upturn'd toward me there, so rigid and white!
O God, my brain reels!—'Tis a dream! My old sight

Is dimm'd with these horrors.—My son! oh, my son!
Would I had died for thee, my own, only one!
There, lift off your arms; let him come to the breast
Where first he was lull'd, with my soul's hymn, to
rest!
Your heart never thrill'd to your lover's fond kiss
As mine to his baby-touch:—was it for *this?*

He was yours too; he loved you! Yes, yes, you're right!
Forgive me, my daughter: I'm madden'd to-night!
Don't moan so, dear child: you're young, and your
years
May still hold fair hopes—but the old die of tears!
Yes, take him again! ah,—don't lay your face *there!*
See, the blood from his wound has stain'd your loose
hair.

How quiet you are!—Has she fainted?—her cheek
Is cold as his own.—Say a word to me,—speak!
Am I crazed?—Is she dead?—Has *her* heart broke
first?
Her trouble was bitter, but sure mine is worst!—
I'm afraid! I'm afraid! alone with these dead!—
Those corpses are stirring! God help my poor head!

I'll sit by my children until the men come
To bury the others, and then we'll go home!
Why, the slain are all dancing!—Dearest, don't move!
Keep away from my boy! he's guarded by love!—
Lullaby, lullaby; sleep, sweet, darling, sleep!
God and thy mother will watch o'er thee keep!

A LETTER FOUND IN A TENT.

I THINK you will not cast aside, nor shred
With your fair fingers and a scornful smile,
This paper into strips, when you shall read
'Twas writ upon the night before I died.
For I shall die to-morrow—the great fight
Comes off at dawn, and my place is in front;
And I am very glad, for I do know
You cannot cast your careless eyes adown
The long list of the slain, and see my name
Without a stir within your heart, a thought
Of how you held my life within your hand
And cast it unto death; you cannot meet
My widow'd mother's face, my sister's grief,
Nor feel your coldness shaken into pain!
And in the solemn silence of the night
Your memories will rise up to slay your sleep,
And with the sting of sharp remorse avenge
My woe upon that woman's soul of yours!

Until at last you see through your own tears
How true, how strong, how earnest was the love
Your calm, proud eyes just glanced at and look'd o'er,
Treading with your slow, imperial step
A man's best hopes into despair's dark dust,
And never listening to the throbbing heart
That beat its wild dreams out beneath your feet!

Ah, well! I did not mean to spend this hour
The last, reproaching you for what is done,
But just to use these moments, while my pulse
Still leaps to fever-heat at thought of you,
To say that I forgive you all the past,—
Forgive you that you watch'd my mad love grow
From birth to passion, from faint, timid hope
To ripe presumption and betraying speech,
And never stoop'd from off the icy throne
Of your self-sway, to free, by word or look,
Your slave from chains of his own high desires,
Until he placed the sword within your grasp
With which you pierced his quivering being through,
Drawing the keen edge of your swerveless will
Against his fate, with your untroubled words,
And sweet, clear voice,—"I cannot love you, sir!"
And so the frenzy of that bitter hour
Dash'd reason off—and I shall lead the van
Upon to-morrow's field, and drown in blood
The worthless life your red lips would not save;
And though you weep not, yet you shall not blush
To know I loved you even unto death!

I think, perhaps, when you shall read these lines,
You will accuse me—for you are not vain—
Of overrating your weak power, and think
That my forgiveness is too overstrain'd
For your offence: 'tis true, you could not give
The blossom of your spirit, till the leaves
Had open'd into bloom; and mine, alas!
Was not the breath its freshness to inhale!
Nor is it well for an immortal soul
To cast the reins of destiny to hands
That have not learn'd to guide wild passion's course;
And I had grown not to that height sublime
Of human victory,—conquest o'er myself!
But eyes that catch a shadow from the wings
Of God's great angel win prophetic sight;
And I can see among the coming years
A time when, living with your idols crush'd,
Your wounded heart, you shall look sadly back
Upon my sorrow, that you scarce heed now,
And think your pain a retribution sent
By justice for your girlhood's deed; and then
It may bring comfort to your stricken soul
To feel that I forgave you ere you died,—
Forgave and loved you so that when you come
Into the world beyond, and meet me there,
Waiting for you alone, with your deep need
Of love still unfulfill'd in earth or heaven,
And say, with yearning eyes, "But only thou
Gave me the spirit's truest love in life,

And I am lonely, wanting it, e'en here!"
Why, I at last shall take you in my arms
And kiss that curving mouth! Till then, adieu!

THE CURSE OF THE GRAPE.

Over the shadows made by the vine,
  Under the arches of twining green,
Pendent and purple the clusters glow,
  With rifts of sunlight sparkling between.
The gatherers, poising on graceful heads
  Their laden baskets, pass gayly there,
Laughing, singing, till the full-juiced fruit
  Trembles with ripeness on cadenced air.

The vintage song 'neath the cloudless skies
  Rings free from a tone of woe or pain;
But, alas! with moans of broken hearts
  It echoes back to those lands again!
The golden and ruby streams of wealth
  Out of the wine-press in rich floods pour,
To drown, in their Circean, dancing foam,
  Dearest hopes and dreams the wide world o'er!

Sing, bacchanals, at your noisy feasts!
  Sing, harvesters, in your vintage bowers!
Crown your god with wreath of freshest leaves!
  Deck your groaning wains with fairest flowers!

Through all the music and all the mirth,
 Yearns up the heavens an anguish'd cry,
From slaves that line the triumphant path
 As Juggernaut's car is passing by!

Accursed! Those globes of nectarine dew
 Bear mid their beauty the serpent's trail;
The lives that crush them on eager lips
 Must hear in their soul the seraph's wail!
Accursed! accursed! the hearth and the hall
 Hurl back on the grape their deepest hate!
Vintners, beware! in each luscious branch
 The demons for some lost spirit wait.

AN EXPERIENCE.

I STOOD one morning, in the soften'd light,
 Before a great man's thought, made clear to mine
By all the wealth of color and rich art,
 The harmony of grace and rare design.

I felt its truth dawn slowly on my brain,
 Until its fulness swell'd the fount of tears,
And, looking through the canvas, I beheld
 Prophetic glimpses of the coming years;

And for an instant felt myself allied
 In inspiration to that artist mind
That thus, mid daily life, in simple things
 The spell of beauty could forever find.

The exaltation of my spirit grew
  Akin to pain, as overflowing eyes
Drew curious stares, half smiling to behold
  Prim custom's screen from uncheck'd feeling rise.

And so I pass'd into the noisy street,
  The brilliant sunshine, and the busy throng,
As one half waken'd from delicious dream
  Hears mingling with rude tones an angel's song.

"How poor," my gathering senses inly said,
  "How barren all these narrow lives appear!
How low their means, how little their desires!
  How pride and glitter win their reverence here!

"While souls like that great painter's stand apart,
  Sublime by inspiration, and their power
To sway the higher instincts of the herd,
  And hold them fetter'd for a passing hour!

"Surely these few, the sovereigns of the world,
  Are nearer God, and see His throne more plain,
Than all these shallow vendors in the mart,
  Whose dearest hopes are those of self and gain!"

Just then another inward voice replied,
  "Be still, O judging heart; for what art thou
Darest call God's creatures common and unclean,
  And makest idols where thy soul may bow?

"The lowest being in yon restless crowd
In Heaven's sight is as the grandest great,
Their breath a thought of God: the mysteries hid
Of birth and death give all an equal state!

"And every man holds that within himself
No other man may know! Alas! 'tis not
The gifted only that do stand alone
And yearn and weep: it is the common lot!

"For though we sit together at the feast,
And pledge each other's secret hope or plan,
And tell the stories of our different fates,
And think we know at last our neighbor man;

"And though we feel the clasp of tender arms,
And walk through bitter trials hand in hand,
And lean on hearts that love has made our own,
And side by side near open graves do stand;

"Yet evermore within each separate soul
Is that can be interpreted aright
By One alone, the everlasting God,
That weighs our actions by our inner light!

"And they, the mighty ones that work apart,
Children of Genius, are servants sent,
Evangels to their brethren, and their gifts
Are but the Sender's means a short space lent!

"They are the priests that go behind the veil
Of flesh and sense, and, standing face to face
With God's own glory, bring His word again
To listening people from the holy place!

"They rouse the Possible in human minds;
They lift to heaven low and grovelling dreams;
They bear the truth to earnest, seeking hearts;
On darken'd souls let in sweet beauty's gleams!

"This is *their* mission; let each one take heed
To act his own in justice and in faith,
Lest, it may be, the Nature scorn'd on earth
May soar the highest in the hour of death!"

A PERUVIAN'S ADDRESS TO THE SUN, AFTER THE CONQUEST.

O SUN, slow sinking in the summer sky,
Tinging the western clouds to glory's glow,
While round about thee purple islands lie,
And over crimson'd peaks thy last rays flow!
Thy silent radiance recalls those days
My nation worshipp'd thee! when temples grand
Thine image held, and reverent songs of praise
Greeted, each dawn, thy rising o'er the land!
When kings the title of thy children bore,
And all the people knew of good and bright

Was deem'd from thee, or shining semblance wore
  To one great source of beauty, warmth, and light!

No longer now, on golden symbols shed,
  Thy beams awaken holy morning hymn!
The virgins from thy sacred halls are fled!—
  And yet thy dazzling splendor grows not dim!
The cruel stranger treads our conquer'd shore,
  The Inca blood cries out to thee in wrath,
And helpless slaves thy mercies loud implore!—
  Yet calm thy course upon thy lustrous path!
O Sun, O mighty god! veil o'er thy face!
  Shed dreadful darkness o'er this wretched land,
To hide the ravage of the white man's trace:
  With vengeful terror strike this fearless band!

Their priests do tell us of a God more great,
  That hearken'd to His servants' earnest cry,
And bade e'en thee amid the heavens wait
  Until His chosen race saw foemen fly,—
The one Pachacamac that rules unseen!
  The true Creator that form'd thee and me!
Whose only sacrifice is hearts made clean!
  Who changes not to all eternity!
They preach Him thus; but evil are their deeds;
  Nor were *we* always pure 'neath thy fair beams.
Their God is most sublime, though base their needs!
  O Sun, shine on: new truth upon me gleams!

1863.

STANZAS,

Suggested by Miss Cushman's Farewell to the Stage.

When Siddons left the sadden'd stage,
  And laid the tragic sceptre down;
And Kemble changed for bridal veil
  The lustre of the drama's crown;
Melpomene kept lonely state,
  Or cover'd o'er offended eyes,
As new aspirants seized her robes
  And bade reluctant curtains rise.

But Heaven at last, that will not be
  Without a witness of its power,
Jove's mourning daughter saw, and gave
  Another bright, auspicious hour!
For one amid the honor'd scenes
  Of Shakspeare reign'd a queen supreme,
Brought life once more to storied shapes,
  A spirit to the poet's dream!

The wondering Muse her buskin loosed,
  And bound it on the foot that trod
Wide realms of passion with the power
  Of priestess guided by a god.
She placed her dagger in this hand,
  And yielded up her regal throne,
To wander in Castalia's shades,
  While Cushman ruled o'er Art alone!

But now the stage again beholds
  Its sovereign abdicate her sway!
The Muse must weep, the world deplore;
  Her brow is weary of its bay.
Yet still within a happy home
  Dear friends will speak her worshipp'd name,
And love shall give her woman heart
  More true content than shouts of fame!

THE REAPERS' RETURN HOME.

(Painted by Becker.)

THROUGH the golden tints of sunset,
  'Neath the glowing, crimson'd skies,
With each smiling face uplifted,
  Where their work's warm flush still lies,
All the reapers, homeward going,
  In a happy, cheerful throng,
With gay voices sing the chorus
  Of an olden harvest-song.

They have mow'd the waving glory
  Of the ripe and bending grain,
Have knelt down where summer's splendor
  Mid the aisle of sheaves has lain,
And have gather'd up the richness
  Of the small seed sown before,

Then with glad eyes stood rejoicing
  In the sure and garner'd store.

Now they onward walk together
  Through the green and pleasant field,
And each worker like a sceptre
  His sharp, shining scythe doth wield;
While the matrons toss their infants
  To the measure of the tune,
Maidens, wishing o'er their shoulders,
  Watch the dim, new-rising moon.

There are glances shy and tender
  Under manly, sunburn'd brows;
There are blushings at bold whispers,
  And fresh murmurs of old vows;
There are laughters, free and ringing,
  Plucking flowers by the way,
And fond clinging of hands parted
  By their labor all the day.

Age and youth and careless childhood
  Share the music of the strain,
As they wend through clover fragrance
  Towards their waiting homes again,
Where the night unto the weary
  Will give slumber without dreams,
And bring silence with deep shadows,
  Till another morning beams.

There is reaping, there is gathering
  For us all upon the earth,
And the sheaves we show at harvest
  Is what proves each spirit's worth!
Let us do our work so bravely
  That our hearts shall sing with praise
In the glow of heaven's glory
  At the closing of our days!
When we lie down for our resting
  In our last home dark and still,
May each tried soul find its waking
  Where Truth's rays the mansions fill!

MERCY'S DREAM.

(Painted by Huntington.)

A WOMAN sleeping in a "lonely place,"
  With lovely brow uplifted for the crown
An angel, floating upon rainbow wings,
  In light and glory brings from heaven down.
And this is all the picture, yet our souls,
  By marvellous skill enwrapt, see more than this:
We watch the seraph take the maiden's hand
  And lead her through the golden doors of bliss;
We follow them, mid brightness like the sun,
  To where, on great white throne, One sits supreme,

And hear the "Welcome, daughter!" caught by
strains
That thrill through Paradise and Mercy's Dream!

We think, perchance, the air about us now
Is full of these angelic shapes, that wait
Till we bemoan the hardness of our hearts
Ere they can whisper "Peace" near Eden's gate!
Their unseen radiance may round us shine
When we are weary in a lonely place,
And in a seeming sleep our souls may go
Close to God's throne with them, and see his face!
And if, like Mercy, with pure love we tread
Among our fellows this dark earth beneath,
Our deeds shall draw down angels from the skies,
And glow like jewels in our heavenly wreath!

A SUMMER'S MEMORY OF BERKSHIRE, MASS.

(Painted by Jas. M. Hart.)

A LOVELY vale, shut in by solemn hills,
Where purple mists, great Nature's incense, rise
To meet the fleecy clouds that float o'er fields
Where brooding peace mid lengthening shadows
lies;
A shallow brook that foams o'er brown, bare stones,
In whose clear waters laving cattle stand;

A waiting wain high heap'd with fragrant hay,
  And sense of summer spread through all the land!

This is an artist's "memory"! O'er his soul
  The viewless spirit of this silent scene
Shed inspiration, that its haunt might win
  Immortal freshness for a season's green!
And so, upon our winter's gloomy verge,
  A fair, warm picture of past glory lives,
That mid earth's coldness and white, coming snows
  The very essence of dead summer gives!

Keeps not each human heart some vision bright,
  On life's long journey, of a cherish'd place
Wherein yet waves hope's golden, unreap'd grain,
  And love still wears its rich, unfaded grace?
Where soar high aspirations unto heaven,
  While barren rocks are veil'd in tinted haze,
Youth's sweetest dream, our being's vale of rest,
  A summer memory of dear, perish'd days!

November, 1863.

ITALIA.

(Painted by Merle.)

Amid the ruins of her splendors past,
  On throne of sorrows does Italia sit,
While ghosts of glories and grand regal state
    Before her memory flit.

She lists no longer shouts of triumphs ring,
Whose haughty echoes made the nations pale;
But through her vinelands, from the grave of hope,
Goes up a people's wail.

With eyes of yearning, and droop'd, clasping hands,
She now looks outward, and awaits a fate,
Lonely and sadden'd, but more loved and fair
Than they whom strength makes great.

Her grapes are purple on her thousand hills;
Her skies are cloudless; and the golden glow
Of noon and sunset fills the air with light
Where days like dreams do flow.

Her stones are storied; heroes form her dust;
She holds rare jewels in undying fames;
And classic ages call to passing times
Her soil bears still their names.

Art's home is with her; and white, peerless shapes
Still bring the wide world's tribute to their grace;
While her old painters, with dead, stirless hands,
Touch earth's most distant place.

Yet mid her treasures does she mournful stay,
The tyrant's captive, who was once a queen,
While despots quarrel o'er the weeping prize,
And Freedom flies the scene.

O crush'd Italia, weak from many ills,
  Thine hour is dawning, thy hard chains shall break!
For strong Opinion, like a Samson bound,
    Begins from sleep to wake!

And men remember what thou wert of yore,
  While Europe's pulses with war's heat are stirr'd;
And thou shalt hear, amid the battle-cries,
    Thy resurrection-word!

And, clad in beauty, lift thy head once more
  Among the crown'd ones, with thine ancient song,
"Io triumphus! Io triumphus!
    Italia rights her wrong!"

April, 1864.

LEGENDS OF THE ROUND TABLE.

NOTE.

SEVERAL years before reading a line of Tennyson, I had met with the old romance of "Prince Arthur," translated from the French. Observing then the poetical nature of many of its incidents, I selected for future experiment most of those which afterwards formed the groundwork of these legends; though some—"The First Meeting of Launcelot and Guinevere," "The King and the Bard," and "Avilion"—had their origin entirely in my own imagination. The first six of the series were printed in the "Evening Journal" of Philadelphia, in 1857; the next two were published in 1859, before the appearance of "Idylls of the King;" the rest were written since, with the exception of "The Best Knight," and "The Last Meeting of Launcelot and Guinevere," which were composed more than a year before, though not issued in the "Home Journal" of New York until some time after Tennyson's book came out.

This explanation is furnished so as to exonerate myself from an anticipated accusation of plagiarism of idea.

SALLIE BRIDGES.

EXCALIBUR.

For months it rested in the stone,
  The sword Excalibur;
The noblest knights of England's realm
  Strove hard the steel to stir;
For word had gone through all the land
  That he who drew the blade
Should fill the sovereign's empty throne,
  The rightful king be made.

The flower of island chivalry
  Had come from far and near,
To try their skill at tournament
  The first day of the year.
Mid the barons went Sir Ector,
  His valiant son, Sir Kaye,
And his foster-child, young Arthur,
  Forth to the courtly fray.

Unknown to all, dead Uther's son
  Mix'd with the noble throng,
Who dream'd not that to stripling page
  Could crown and throne belong.
"Now, grammercy," quoth Arthur,
  In riding by Sir Kaye,
"Good brother mine, how came you out
  Without a sword to-day?"

Sir Kaye look'd down, and paled to see
No weapon at his side:
Then back his comrade spurr'd his steed,
Across the meadows wide,
To where lay idle in its sheath
The knight's forgotten blade,
But found that not a single squire
Had in the castle stay'd.

Quoth Arthur then, with sudden wrath,
"From yonder mystic stone
I'll pluck the sword, that good Sir Kaye
May wield it as his own!"
So, lighting down from off his horse,
Towards the empty tent
In which was kept Excalibur
His eager footsteps bent.

Its golden-letter'd hilt was bright,
Its knightly guards away;
And so, with brave and fearless heart,
He made his bold essay.
He grasp'd the handle in his hand,
Its point leap'd sharp and free.
"My brother shall not go unarm'd
To battle now!" cried he.

When old Sir Ector saw the blade
Flash in the morning light,

He knew it was the Sword of Fate
  That met his wondering sight,
And ask'd of Arthur, "Whither came
  The steel thou gavest Sir Kaye?"
"I bore it," was the plain reply,
  "From stone and tent away."

"Then, by my faith," the gray knight swore,
  "An' thou canst draw again
The sword from out the selfsame place,
  A monarch thou shalt reign!"
And back within the marble stone
  Prince Arthur thrust the blade,
While long in vain to pluck it thence
  Both high and low essay'd.

"Come hither; strive again, my son!"
  And quick on Ector's sight,
In Arthur's hand, the marvellous steel
  Was flashing keen and bright.
Then kneel'd Sir Ector and Sir Kaye,
  With every squire and lord,
To greet as lawful king the youth
  Who lean'd upon the Sword!

Then spoke his aged foster-sire,
  "Ye hail no child of mine!"
But wist not buried Uther's heir
  Was king by right divine.

Thus Arthur through Excalibur
Received his father's crown;
And ever through Excalibur
He kept his high renown!

THE DEATH OF LANCEOR.

The fight was over, and one shiver'd spear
Had dash'd to splinters 'gainst a coat of mail;
The other, crushing an opposing shield,
Had pierced the hauberk of a valiant knight
And let his brave life through a ghastly rent.
Upon the green hill-side Sir Lanceor fell,
No more in tournament or joust to strive;
And good Sir Balin gazed upon his foe,
And sadden'd that his hand had stretch'd him there,
Albeit in self-defence each blow was struck:
Yet well he knew he might not often meet,
In field or tourney, opponent so bold!
And while he lean'd upon his unsheathed sword,
Resting a moment after contest fierce,
Sudden from out the forest at his side
A fair, white palfrey, galloping with speed,
Bore to his feet a damsel full of grace,
Who, when she saw Sir Lanceor thus slain,
Alighted down, and made a tearful wail,
Clasping her arms about the stirless form,
Casting on Balin each upbraiding look,

Wounding his soul with frantic words of woe:
"Ah! not one life alone hast thou destroy'd,
Thou cruel knight that slew this love of mine!
Two hearts thy weapon shatter'd when it cast
This stalwart body on the trampled turf!"
She took the steel from out the dead man's hand,
And swoon'd in freeing thence the stiffen'd grasp;
And when she lifted up her pallid face,
All tear-bedew'd and framed in golden curls,
Sir Balin's thought was grieving passing sore
That thus his act should make a lady's dole.
He strove the slender fingers to untwine
From round the heavy hilt of Lanceor's blade;
But, lightly stepping from his careful hold,
Quickly she set the pommel on the ground,
And thrust her bosom on the shining point.
The ruby blood came gushing from her wound,
Like red wine spill'd from goblet made of pearl;
The gentle figure, white-enrobed, sank down,
Like to a stricken dove upon its nest;
The violet eyes reproach'd him for her death,
Then closed forever on her lover's breast.
Oh, matchless love of woman! Sure thou art
The only flower of Eden left to bloom
Amid the thorny thistles of real life,
Scenting the wayside with thy rich perfume,
Brightening with beauty common spots of earth!
"Alas!" said Balin, looking on the pair,
"Sorely repent I now this brave knight's death,
Because of her who loved him living so!

And yet methinks 'twere happiness to die,
In armor clad, doing one's right devoir,
With one we love to breathe their last, warm sigh
In sorrow out, surviving not our loss!"
While thus he mused aloud, on horseback came,
Riding apace, a dwarf from Camelot,
That wildly grieved above the lifeless twain.
Quoth good Sir Balin, "'Twas a sorry deed;
And yet himself gave challenge for the tilt!
No craven heart is mine to fly from foe,
And fate had will'd that one should linger here.
The damsel died for love of yon still knight,
And evermore I hold, for her sweet sake,
All womankind in highest, dear esteem!"
As thus they talk'd, King Mark of Cornwall rode
On gallant charger by the touching group,
And sorrow'd greatly for such true hearts dead,
Swearing with vows he would not stir from thence
Till he had raised above their dust a tomb.
Then, pitching his pavilion on the spot,
His squires sought through all the country round
To find a sepulchre would shrine them both;
And ere Sir Balin took his parting leave
Of Cornwall's generous sovereign, he had reared,
A monument right passing rich and fair,
Brought from some distant church, and rarely carved
And sculptured on the stone their name and fate:—
"Here lieth Lanceor, a valiant knight,
Prince Arthur's friend, and son of Ireland's king,
Kill'd by Sir Balin of the Table Round,

In lawful tilt upon the green hill-side;
And on his breast the ladye of his love
Sleepeth till judgment, slain by her own hand,
For very sorrow, with her lover's sword!
Pray for the souls, O gentle passer-by,
Of fair Colombe and brave Sir Lanceor!"

THE TOMB OF THE TWELVE KINGS.

Within St. Steven's holy aisle,
Requiems chanting all the while,
They buried bold King Lot.
Right bravely he had fought, and well:
Minstrel and harper long could tell
How fatally his sharp strokes fell
Ere his own death was got!

With dripping sword and shatter'd mail,
He shower'd blows without avail
To turn the battle's tide;
His best knights lay around him, slain;
His wounded steed was mad with pain;
Twelve kings a bloody couch had ta'en,
And slumber'd side by side!

No recreant he, to turn and fly:
So, shouting loud his battle-cry,
He charged Sir Pellinore!

The knight heaved once his ruddy blade,
One downward stroke the weapon made,
That ever still the monarch laid,
His life and warfare o'er!

And when the hour of strife was done,
Prince Arthur bade the knights who won
Bear forth the gallant dead,
And foremost in the funeral train
To place that valiant sovereign slain,
That first in field by him again
His comrades might be led!

And then within the sacred walls,
Their tatter'd banners for their palls,
And sword in each right hand,
They buried them at Camelot;
And Arthur built upon the spot
Their tomb, to keep still unforgot
The fame of this brave band!

In sepulchre full rich and fair,
Of marble stone with carving rare,
They laid King Lot alone;
And where the other sovereigns lay,
Twelve gilded figures, night and day,
Held burning tapers bright alway
Above their tablet stone.

And over all, with unsheathed sword,
Stood Arthur as their conquering lord,
 The crown upon his head!
For years before the Sancgreal came,
Above each quaintly sculptured name,
Like living bursts of golden flame,
 Their light the tapers shed.

THE FIRST MEETING OF SIR LAUNCELOT AND QUEEN GUINEVERE.

The Lady Guinevere was crown'd,
And all Prince Arthur's Table Round
 Their fealty came to yield.
She sat, the very fairest queen
That England's realm had ever seen,
Beside the bravest king, I ween,
E'er handled weapon sharp and keen
 Or sceptre learn'd to wield.

The golden circlet jewell'd rare
Shone through the wealth of braided hair
 That wreathed her perfect head;
With crimson robe and snowy vest,
And gems on arms and rounding breast,
It seem'd to every knightly guest
To be a hope supremely blest
 For her his blood to shed.

As one by one their bearded lips
Just press'd her slender finger-tips,
  In token of their zeal,
She bore her part with regal grace,
That show'd the throne was fitting place
For blood of Leodegraunce's race;
And who before such peerless face
  Would hesitate to kneel?

But when, unhelmeted and tall,
Sir Launcelot trode across the hall
  And bow'd before the throne,
A sudden meeting of their eyes
Quick caused the eddying blood to rise,
To flush her cheek with richer dyes,
Each echoing the other's sighs,
  As his hand touch'd her own.

And thus, an instant, all forgot
Was royal mien and queenly lot
  In joy of passion's birth;
The heart-pulse leapt through all her frame;
Love's dawning broke in rosy flame
Of blushing clouds that went and came
As Launcelot vow'd henceforth her name
  Should be his star on earth!

A moment, and the spell was o'er:
The *woman* was a queen once more,
  And Launcelot, loyal knight;

But ever through that festal day,
Mid tournament or mock-mêlée,
Their glances caught each other's ray;
And Arthur praised her that alway
Her blushes were so bright!

MERLIN'S GRAVE.

Mighty wizard was old Merlin, the wisest of his age;
But Love all living men subdues, and Love spared not the sage:
So the gray-beard grew a dotard for one fair woman's sake,
Ever following and wooing the Ladye of the Lake;
For she chain'd him with her beauty, and ruled him with a smile,
Till he taught her each enchantment, each magic charm and wile;
And on the four Evangelists an oath she made him swear
That his subtle craft should never her life with mysteries snare.

But she loved no whit the wizard: yet, to learn his mystic art,
She feign'd a loving passion, and acted well her part;
And he taught her all the wonders of the fire, earth, and sea,
All the marvels of the genii, all tricks of glamourie,

Gave her words of spell and power the spirits to command,
And gifted her with prophecy, with lore from every land.
But she wearied of the master when his parables were o'er,
And ladies laugh at lovers gray-bearded and three-score.

Thus it happen'd, as they journey'd, he show'd her by the way,
Mid a rock, a deep-hewn cavern, wherein a wonder lay,
But that hitherto was hidden beneath a weighty stone
From the entrance could be shaken by sorcery alone;
Then she pray'd the old magician, with many a witching word,
To venture in and record bear what sights were there interr'd:
In an evil hour for Merlin he did the Ladye's will,
For she quickly wrought her magic, and the rock entombs him still.

Long in court and council-chamber they waited for the sage,
And marvell'd what endeavor his absence should engage;

'Twas whisper'd he had wander'd afar beyond the main
To countries of the Orient, and yet would come again,
With more than mortal wisdom, to work for England's weal,
From the sepulchre of Solomon bearing home the sacred seal.
But forever kept the Ladye the secret of the stone,
As she sat beneath the waters and wrought her spells alone.

SIR LAUNCELOT'S SLUMBER.

THE golden sunshine gemm'd the stream,
Where drooping lilies shadows made;
The willow-branches touch'd the wave,
As though they woo'd their own cool shade;
A Sabbath stillness fill'd the air;
The very insects ceased their tones;
Only the waters rippling by
Made music round gray, sunken stones.

The river-road was hot and dry;
Beyond, a broad, green meadow lay,
Wherein was set a single tree,
Whose ripening fruit perfumed the way;

Its clustering leaves and laden limbs
  Darken'd below the grassy plain,
While o'er its gnarl'd and rugged roots
  Naturo a mossy cloak had lain.

Adown the scorch'd and pebbled road
  Sir Launcelot came this summer morn
With glittering hauberk, glaives of steel,
  And lance upon his saddle borne.
He left the pathway, cross'd the field,
  And 'neath the spreading apple-tree
Unarm'd his weary, mail-clad steed,
  And let him roam the pasture free.

Unloosing then his visor'd casque,
  Upon the sward he downward laid,
His helm for pillow, and his hand
  Clasping the pommel of his blade.
Thus slumber'd he at noontide hour,
  The bravest knight in all the world,
With stalwart form and sunburn'd brow,
  Where, all untrain'd, the brown hair curl'd.

And as, perchance, in daring dreams,
  He spent the rapture of a kiss
On Guinevere's red, dewy lips,
  And felt their softness cling to his,
Four lovely queens, on four white mules,
  Rode slowly through the meadow green,
O'er whom four knights on lifted spears
  Bore canopy of silken sheen.

And as they wended on their way,
  Sudden there burst upon their sight,
Dreaming beneath the golden fruit,
  This vision of a sleeping knight.
And, gathering round his grassy couch,
  In earnest whispers spoke each dame,
Disputing which could love him most,
  And which the captive's self should claim.

But Morgan Le Fay, of Gore the Queen,
  A ladye subtle, proud, and wise,
Then wrought a spell of glamour old,
  That bound the poppies on his eyes,
Until within her castle near
  Their knights had borne him o'er the field,
His hand still clasp'd upon his sword,
  And he outstretch'd on his own shield.

And there she woke him from the spell;
  And, when the morrow's sun was bright,
All richly dress'd, the four fair queens
  Assail'd the heart of this brave knight,—
King Arthur's sister, false Le Fay,
  The Ladye of the North Countrie,
Eastland's proud queen, and she who ruled
  The isles upon a distant sea.

But still the pleasure of his dream
  Thrill'd through Sir Launcelot's waking hour;
Before the image of his love
  All other charms had lost their power;

And so he hearken'd not their speech,
  Or answer'd them with careless tone,
Till each, enraged, withdrew her suit,
  And left him with his thoughts alone.

There is no cause like this on earth
  To rouse a woman's slumbering ire,
To turn her fondest love to hate,
  And kindle pride's enduring fire:
Crush her, condemn, insult, abuse,
  She ne'er forsakes, and still loves on;
But scorn, neglect, and passion's slave,
  She vengeance seeks, her patience gone!

And so they kept Sir Launcelot there,
  A prisoner, many a weary day,
Rust gathering on his armor bright,
  He chafing at his idle stay.
But never once, in word or deed,
  His sworn allegiance shook or swerved;
At Guinevere's fair shrine alone
  He worshipp'd still, and Arthur served.

But when the queens relax'd a while
  Their constant watch and steadfast guard,
Forth to his olden freedom then,
  Through twelve strong locks, twelve gates close-barr'd,
A damsel guided him once more,
  To battle for her father's sake;
And boldly was that promise kept
  By good Sir Launcelot of the Lake.

BEAUMAINS' VOW.

'Twas Whitsunday morn, and King Arthur held
  Round Table at Kenedon Hall,
But vowed at Pentecost never to eat
  Till adventure strange should befall.
So his hundred and fifty armèd knights
  Sat patiently waiting at noon,
And only Sir Launcelot murmur'd aloud,
  "God send meat and adventure soon!"

But sudden and curious silence fell,
  As enter'd the door of the hall
Two men, on whose shoulders another lean'd,
  Fair-handed, well-visaged, and tall,
And spoke to the king, as he rear'd him straight,
  "My monarch, I come here to pray
Three gifts of thy grace; but of only one
  I crave the fulfilment to-day."

"We grant thy demand," the sovereign said:
  "Sure thine is some lofty desire."
"But meat and drink for a year," he replied.
  "Faith!" cried Arthur, "a valiant squire!
So strong as thou seemest, why askest not
  For knighthood, armor, or steed?
Such hand as thine could Excalibur wield;
  And is food thine uttermost need?"

"'Tis all I now wish: for mine other boons
I will sue at next Whitsuntide."
And the knights all sneer'd, as they broke their fast,
"More size has the varlet than pride."
Sir Kaye, the steward, in mocking despite,
Gave him place where the lackeys ate;
And only Sir Gawaine and Launcelot swore
That his mien was of nobler state.

The twain were right; for when Arthur again
The Pentecost holyday kept,
When adventure rare claim'd the bravest heart,
'Twas this Beaumains forward stept,
And boldly implored two boons of the king.
The first was this perilous quest;
And then that Sir Launcelot should dub him knight.
Quoth Sir Launcelot, "Not without test."

From the palace forth went the royal chief,
With his mail'd and warrior train,
To witness Sir Launcelot and Beaumains try
A tilt on the tournament-plain.
Short joust did they hold; for the far-famed knight
Had sore work to keep him unshamed.
"'Twas right gallantly fought," said the king and lords,
As the stranger the promise claim'd.

Then, spurr'd and belted, he mounted his horse,
With Sir Launcelot's sword on his thigh;

For Sir Launcelot learn'd, ere the accolade,
His name, kin, and lineage high.
And little the haughty Sir Gawaine deem'd,
As Sir Gareth rode proudly away,
That his brother had kept a vow unbroke
At court for a year and a day.

THE KING AND THE BARD.

"Come, sing us a lay!" quoth Arthur,
"My Bard of the Table Round!
Some ballad of lofty courage,
That shall make our heart's-blood bound!"
And the monarch drain'd his goblet,
While the minstrel tuned his lyre,
And fill'd it again, that the singer
Might win from wine new fire.

"Now drink," said the generous sovereign,
"That, when thy song shall be o'er,
We may fill with bright gold pieces
And hand thee the cup once more."
But the minstrel's voice was silent,
And the ruby wine undrain'd,
While Arthur, impatient, wondered
Why the guerdon was not gain'd".

The bard from his seat rose slowly,
  And spoke to the waiting king:
"Sire, to-day my soul is tuneless,
  And no worthy lay can sing.
Not e'en for your tempting liquor,
  Not e'en for your promised gold,
Will my inner voice yield music;
  For true song cannot be sold!

"But when fitting words can utter
  Dreams that stir my own deep heart,
In thine shall the chords re-echo,
  Till it feels of mine a part.
Not till inspiration smiteth
  On the rock of silent Thought,
Can be welcome living waters
  To the king or people brought!"

"Thou art right!" the sovereign answer'd;
  "'Tis a lesson nobly told:
Monarchs cannot rule men's *spirits*
  By the might of law or gold!
Thou art first of all my minstrels,
  Thou art best of Britain's boast;
But take now my brimming goblet,
  And quaff it to Arthur's toast.

"Drink, gallant knights, to the minstrel
  Who dreads neither prince nor peer,—
Who can speak the truth to power,
  Nor flatters for price or fear,—

To the bard who freely renders
  The gift he has been given,
And sings but when his strain exalts
  His hearers nigher heaven!"

THE LOVE-DRINK.

King Marke of Cornwall sent Sir Tristan forth,
With goodly company in grand array,
On embassy to Anguish, Ireland's king;
That there his nephew's eloquence might move
The father's heart to give his daughter's hand;
For Marke had heard the minstrels sing of her,
La Belle Isonde, until his throne had seem'd
Empty without a queen, and listen'd then
His people's murmuring that he did not wed;
And so he chose the princess for his bride.

But on the way Sir Tristan met a lord,
With many peers, that in the name of might
Truage of Cornwall did demand with swords!
And Tristan slew him, but did get himself
Such serious hurt, that those about him pray'd
For his soul's rest, and begg'd him but to stay
His journey's progress till his wound was heal'd.
But the brave knight bound up his gaping side,
And bade them onward:—"Duty could not wait

Because a man should bleed! He will'd to live
Until his errand was all done, and then—
Why, God's good pleasure should hear his Amen!"

And so he came at last to Ireland's court,
And in the audience-hall, before the throne,
Stood pale and leaning on his sheathéd sword,
And told his message to the king and queen,
Fainting, in ending, at the princess' feet,
Whose tender eyes dropp'd tears amid the blood
That gush'd afresh, as trembling she essay'd
To quench its flowing with her own warm scarf;
And, as she was well skill'd in surgery's art,
They gave him to her charge to try his cure.
And long she wrestled with the angel Death,
Conquering through prayer, and won him back to
life.
And Tristan watch'd her from his couch, and wish'd
He might be ill forever, thus to keep
So fair a picture always in his sight!
And she would do for him, with quiet grace,
All offices that only women can,
When, smote by sickness, men will humbly lean
On the strong tenderness that never fails!
The little hand smooth'd pillows for his head,
Bathed his hot brow, and dress'd his healing wound,
And, when he seem'd to slumber mid his pain,
Plied silken threads to aid her silent watch.
And if sometimes it met his own, 'twas but
The leech's touch to learn the fever's height.

And all about, within her was such sense
Of maiden purity, that Tristan ne'er,
Even by thought of passion, would have stirr'd
Th' unconscious calm of that white, virgin breast!

So day by day he grew to perfect health,
And, sitting by her in the summer morns,
He taught her how to tune the lute, and sang
Old ditties, mostly battle-songs, or lays
Of sunny France, the harvest-hymns, or plaints
Of captive slaves,—but never sang of love!
And if her changing cheek did flush and pale,
And her heart throb, she knew 'twas but the tunes,
The music shaking all her inner soul;
And if she did not laugh as she was wont,
But from the castle-terrace gazed long hours
Toward distant Cornwall, all her maids would say,
"She's sad because she leaves us: this quick change
From home to husband weighs her spirits down.
She wonders if he'll love her like her sire!
He must be noble, since the knights he sent
Are gentle, and his herald like a king.
She's worn with watching. Sure her lord may count
Upon the goodness that did patient nurse
The proxy for his sake will call her queen!"
And so they gossip'd on her alter'd ways,
And—for they knew her all her girlhood up—
Did never link her name, by sneer or hint,
In thought or speech, with aught that was not true.

And thus, with this fine honor in them both,
That knew her pledged, they kept them safe through
all;
And if perchance o'er Tristan's soul would come
A sudden tempting, when she stept anear,
To seize her in his arms, and kiss her eyes,
Mouth, hands, once strain her to his heart, and then
Tear open his old wound, and pitied die,
He sternly fought it down, and school'd his thought
To say, unshrinkingly, "My uncle's wife!"

And when their ship was ready, all the court
Did bear her company to the water's edge,
And the whole country mourn'd to see her go.
She wept to know how she was loved,—to leave
Her childhood's happy home for stranger roof,—
To see no more, perchance, the early friends
That fill'd her memory; and all sights and sounds
Seem'd but to make her sadder as she went,
Until she look'd on Tristan, and her heart
Took a sweet sense of something undefined,
That made her think but of the voyage with him,
Forgetful of the king would crown its end!
And, ere they sail'd, her mother gave in charge
Secretly to Governale, Sir Tristan's squire,
A golden flask full of enchanted wine,
That, on the day when they should wed, King Marke
And her Isonde should drink the same, and so
Either should other love through all their life,
And find expression by its potent spell.

The August days were languid on the sea;
The vessel linger'd on the glassy calm
Of heaveless waves; and, as they silent sate,
Watching from cabin-window a lone bird
Skimming the surface of the waters blue,
Then, more to break the stillness than from need,
Isonde did murmur that she was athirst;
And Tristan rose to search for welcome draught,
And came back, smiling, with a golden flask,
And told her how he found it in the case
Where Governale did keep his master's helm;
And so—for such rare liquor fitted not
For lackey's palate, howsoe'er or why
He got and kept it—Tristan pour'd the wine,
And gave the goblet to the ladye's taste,
Who drank it, saying she would pay instead
To the sly squire a good broad piece or two.
And, partly that the odor was so rich,
And partly that his mouth might touch the rim
Whereon her dewy lip had press'd, he too
Drain'd from the goblet love's o'erwhelming power.

For, sitting at her feet, with sudden thrill,
Their long-averted looks did meet at last,
As, scarcely heeding, stole his eager hand
Anear to hers, that trembled to his palm,
The while his other arm about her form
Bow'd down her blushing face towards his own.
Love compass'd them with circumstance; for them
The sea, the sky, were not, nor aught but love,

In that enraptured space when scarce time seem'd
To move, so fast th' unnoted moments flew.
The world was in the circle of their arms,
And their souls mingled in the speechless bliss
That almost grows to pain, and floods the eyes
With causeless tears that break the lofty spell
Of love's pure exaltation, lest the breath
Of the divine in man should waft his soul
So far towards the source that he should pierce
The mysteries of God's secret Paradise.
And, as her bright drops rain'd upon his brow,
He snatch'd her to his heart, and broken words
Restored them unto life,—"Tristan!" "Isonde!"—
And one long kiss seal'd their eternal troth!

THE BEST KNIGHT.

For a great tilt the lists were all array'd;
And in the gallery, beside the queen,
Truncheon in hand, the crown upon his head,
King Arthur sat, the umpire of the joust;
And back and forth upon th' allotted sward
Arm'd knights upon arm'd steeds rode swift and slow,
To try their chargers' mettle, or to gain
From ladies' eyes some longed-for, envied glance;
For each upon his helmet token wore

Of favor won or hoped through gallant deeds;
And there were whisperings round the throne, from lips
Dewy and red, that soon might pale with fear,
Which made the queen smile slyly to her lord.

But, while all waited for the signal trump,
Mid wondering looks, a litter forward came,
Whereon a sick man lay, and at whose side
An aged dame walk'd with a weary step,
And paused before the king, at whose command
The ladye told her story and her quest.
"From Hungary, sire, the last of many sons
To Spanish tournament went bravely forth,
Strong with rare strength and confident with youth,
And there opposed the proudest knight of Spain,
And, ere he slew him, got these seven wounds.
See, sire, how still they bleed!" And Guinevere
Shut from her shuddering sight the crimson drops
That stain'd the matted hair and broider'd quilt,
While Arthur question'd why the wounds were fresh.
"The mother of Sir Alphegus that died
Was a great sorceress, of subtle craft;
And, for her grief was much—God mend her pain!
I would have done the same had I been she
That saw my dear son dead, and had her power!—
She wrought by secret arts her vengeance thus:
Sir Urre should ne'er be well of these deep cuts
Until the world's best knight had search'd his wounds.

And so, to have him heal'd, for seven years
We two have pass'd through all the Christian lands.
Our last hope is in this: if here we fail,
We will go home again, and pray for death!"
And, ere the king could answer, Guinevere—
Who liked no tilt where Launcelot did not ride,
And trembled always at the blows and groans—
Out of her woman's heart, with woman's wit,
Urged that the joust might be postponed a day,
And all the knights prove value on this test,—
A surer trial than with shields and swords,
And more to England's honor, if perchance
The best knight in the world graced Arthur's court!
And Arthur laid the sceptre in her hand,
And said, "Well, be it so! myself the first—
Not thus presuming on my own poor worth,
But to encourage others to the same—
Will touch for this sore evil; and God help
The patient mother to her son's good weal!"
And so the king,—the brave king,—high in heart
And pure in soul, and noble through grand thoughts,
Gently essay'd to close the gaping wounds,
That bled the more for handling, and grew worse,
Till Arthur said,—a sadness in his eyes,—
"Some flaw is in mine acts: some better man
Must wear the name not Britain's king can boast!"
And, rising, took his ermined mantle off
And laid it on the shoulders of the dame,
Who shiver'd in the fresh spring air that bore
The faint, sweet fragrance of some meadow near.

And one by one they came, princes and dukes,
Knights of the Table Round, all famed and tried:
Of the hundred and fifty, ten were gone
Upon their own adventures far from court.
And all the while, with each attempt that fail'd,
The queen had thought of Launcelot, and her heart
Had murmur'd o'er, "The best in all the world!
This honor is for him! Why comes he not?"
For he had sent her private word that morn,
Though he could not be back in time to tilt,
He would be there ere night, to tread with her
One measure ere he dream'd of her last smile.

And now the shades were lengthening on the plain;
Sir Urre grew faint with bleeding, and the knights
That still remain'd untested were but few.
And Guinevere impatient watch'd the scene,
Pale with expectance, anxious with one hope,
Till the last trial left the wounds agape,
And the poor mother bow'd her wither'd face
Upon her son's well hand, and sobb'd with grief;
While all the men look'd silent on, and felt
A sort of pain and shame to see her weep.

Then, as the queen still strain'd her waiting sight,
Her heart's great throb was echoed by a shout,
That gladly broke the stillness with one name;
And, as Sir Launcelot rode within the lists,
The sceptre roll'd from out her nerveless hand
Upon the earth, close to King Arthur's foot,

Who gently said,—nor meant his words to sting,
Haply unconscious of her conscious ill,—
"You hold your royalty but light, my queen!
See how my sceptre is dust-sullied now,
And nigh to blood! I will take back the charge
Those white, small hands were all too weak to
hold."
And, as he knelt in homage, Launcelot deem'd
The blush upon her cheek his welcome back.

And then the sovereign told him of the test,
Bidding him do as all the rest had done;
But the bold knight shrank back, and humbly
spoke,
"My monarch, bid me wield my sword or lance
In equal combat, or 'gainst fearful odds,
And not one foot of ground my foot will yield,
Till bravest prowess wins the battle's end!
But ask me not to try so high a deed
Where all these lords have failed! Though I be
strong
Against my foes, I am but weak 'gainst sin;
For strength is fortune's accident, but worth
Lies in a man's own soul! And what am I,
That I should work a miracle like Christ?
I am not worthy, sire!"
But here there broke
Upon his words the mother's weeping voice,
That plead, for her dear sake who gave him birth,
He yet would grant her hope this one chance more.

And Launcelot could not bear a woman's tears,
But knelt beside the couch, and bow'd his head,
Saying thus secretly in his own heart:
"O Blessed Trinity, I do beseech
Of Thy great mercy, work this grace through me;
Use me for good, that never of myself
May dare to heal another soul's sore ill,
But trust in Thy great power and my faith!"
And here he touch'd the wounds, that sudden closed
Beneath his hand to hurtless scars, that seem'd
As though they had been well for seven years!
And as the happy mother kiss'd his cheek,
And Arthur hail'd him best knight in the world,
Sir Launcelot brush'd aside a sparkling tear,
And Urre of Hungary leap'd from off his couch,
And wound his arm about his healer's neck,
And vow'd to serve him through the life he gave;
While, from the very fulness of her joy,
The queen could keep her still no more, but ask'd,
In playful tone, "What spell Sir Launcelot used?
What magic unto stouter knights unknown?"
And Launcelot simply said, "I pray'd to God!"

THE QUEST OF THE SANCGREAL.

When Merlin's wisdom for the king ordain'd
The Table Round in likeness of the world,
He placed therein the sieges for each knight
Should sit thereat, and prophesied that one
Who there broke bread the Sancgreal should achieve,
Should win the holy vessel that contain'd
The Saviour's blessed blood, that had been brought
To this far land, after that Christ had died,
By Joseph who had given Him his tomb,
And hid away from common sight of men,
Till he should come so worthy of this grace
That all would say but One e'er lived before
As pure from evil and so brave in deed.
And Merlin made a siege where he might sit,
And call'd the name of it "Siege Perilous,"
Marking it next to Launcelot's at the board,
And giving signs should show fulfilment near.

So, ever at the feasts King Arthur held,
They look'd to see a token of the time;
And more than once, elated by good cheer,
Some gallant sir essay'd that empty seat,
But none e'er sat therein but got a hurt;
And years went by, but still the mystic siege
Waited the coming guest for whom was laid
Trencher and goblet as for all the rest.

At Pentecost 'twas custom of the king
To know adventure ere they went to meat;
So, as they whiled away the lagging hours,
One Whitsuntide, upon the river's bank
That runs to Camelot, a marvel came.
For, lo! a great stone floated down the stream,
Wherein was upright stuck a fair, rich sword,
And golden letters in the marble taught
The best knight in the world to take it thence.
Then unto Launcelot spoke the courteous king,
"Brave sir, the blade is yours!" But Launcelot said,
"Not so, my liege: the best knight in the world,
You do forget, is he shall sit unharm'd
Beside me at the feast! And he that strives
To take that sword and fails shall get a wound
Full sore to heal; for, see, its name is writ
In precious stones upon the shining hilt."
And Arthur read, in rays of diamond light,
The one word "Justice," while Sir Gawaine strove,
And then Sir Percivale, to stir the sword;
But both their hands upon the weapon slipp'd,
And stain'd its edge with blood, until the prince
Forbade endeavor more. "For thus," he said,
"My own Excalibur defied all strength,
Until my destined grasp the handle seized.
This too is fix'd by Fate, and he shall wield
Its keenness rightly will be worthy sure
To have us bow our heads to him. And now
Let's in to dine, and toast our unknown peer!"

And, ere each lord was served in his own place,
Came in an aged man, clothed all in white,
And with him a young knight in crimson robed,
Upon whose shoulders hung a mantle furr'd
With royal ermine,—whose beardless visage bore
The smile of innocence, uplifted, calm
With the mild majesty of one who knows
None greater than his equal, yet who feels
His own soul humble in the sight of God.
And silent round the watching forms they walk'd
Until the elder lifted off the cloth
Laid o'er "Siege Perilous," wherein was writ,
In letters bright as stars, that all could see,
The name of "Galahad;" and that young knight
Sat down therein, and show'd no sign of harm,
The while his comrade bless'd him and went forth.
Then bow'd the king to him, and all the knights
Rose up, and gave him welcome with their hands;
And, after they had dined, the monarch spoke:
"Fair sir, I see the scabbard at thy side
Does lack a sword. Without, a marvel waits:
Wouldst win a weapon, and thy rare right prove
To fill that siege? for prophesy has rank'd
Him 'best knight in the world' should sit therein;
And so a stone proclaims that he shall take
The blade therefrom shall bear the same proud
fame!"
Then Galahad and Arthur, side by side,
Went from the palace to the river's bank,
Where in his hand with ease the stranger held

The trial-sword, and slid it in the case
So smoothly that the good king, wondering, said,
"Surely those two were for each other made!"

And after jousting in the meadow's midst,
Whereat Sir Galahad exceeded all,
The court rode quiet back to Camelot;
And, as they sat at supper in a maze
Of listening wonder at this young knight's words,
A sudden thunder crash'd across his speech,
And shook the pillars of the hall; and sounds
Of rushing wings stirr'd through the darkness deep
That rested there an instant; when a light
Six times more clear than beams of noontide sun
Shone o'er them all, and glorified each face,
So that they all upon their neighbors look'd,
Struck dumb with awe, as through the silence rose
Angelic voices; then an odor rich
Fill'd all their senses, and the taste of each
Knew that was long'd for most and liked the best;
While every soul felt such ecstatic joy
That love's great bliss seem'd but the barren type
Of this exceeding rapture; and then came
Their breath once more, and all things look'd the same.
Then whisper'd they into each other's ears
That there had been the Holy Greal of Christ;
Till Gawaine spoke aloud, and took a vow
That, as its blessing came in part to all,
Though fate ordain'd but one should fully win

The dangerous quest, that, just to know again
Such rare, high feeling, he would seek himself
The Sacred Vessel, which perchance if seen,
Its power might waft his soul so far from earth
That it might float into the gate of heaven,
Since but its unseen presence made them seem
Like olden gods at their ambrosial feasts!"
Then rose they all, and with uplifted hands
Echoed Sir Gawaine's oath; and Arthur said,
"This promise smites my heart; for I do know
Such quest will rob me of my dearest friends,
And break the knightly fellowship we keep
So fair and true that all the world admires.
For never king has had such gallant peers;
And never more shall gather at my board
All those who leave me to my sorrow here!
For kings must fret on thrones, while crownless heads
Find Glory's laurel upon danger's field!"

And when the lords had arm'd themselves, they met
In the great court-yard, waiting by their steeds
Until the king had brought the weeping queen
To give their last farewell; and as the sun,
Slow sinking, cast o'er all a golden light,
They stood upon the palace-steps, both clad
In sparkling jewels and their royal robes;
And as, unhelmetted, with gauntlets off,
The knights came singly by to kiss their hands,
The quick sobs broke from Guinevere's fair breast,

And more than once the shining drops fell down
On some bow'd head; while Arthur, pale and sad,
Would take no homage, but with tender clasp
Press'd each to his full heart, and no one spoke.
And when at last Sir Launcelot came anear,
And held the ladye's palm within his own,
She sank, half fainting, on her husband's arm.
So Galahad but touch'd his maiden lips
To fingers cold as ice, that listless hung,
As wearied of the weight of their rich rings.
At last, when crested helmets were all donn'd
And bow'd in parting to the horses' manes,
The knights together through the gateway rode;
And Arthur watch'd them as their mail'd array
Wound down the path, until on burnish'd shields
The sun's last lingering rays no longer glanced,
Then with a sigh bore in the drooping queen.
And there was weeping of the rich and poor
As through the streets of Camelot they rode,
Where many a dame, with voice nigh choked with
tears,
Did send her prayers with that gay cavalcade;
While ever and anon would leave the ranks
A favor'd sir, to catch upon his lance
Some scarf or token of his lady's grace,
Cast off from balconies where fair forms lean'd.
And so they journey'd to a castle's gates
Wherein the lord made cheer, till in the morn
They parted from each other, and all took,
In pairs or singly, their own different roads.

When many days had gone, Sir Gawaine met
Sir Ector in the way, and both reveal'd
That, after wandering long in beaten paths,
Neither had found adventure that had seem'd
To bring them nearer to the Holy Greal.
"In sooth," quoth Gawaine, "I am weary now
Of this new quest, and loath to follow it."
"And so," said Ector, "all the knights I saw
Upon my travels do complain the same.
Nor can I hear of Launcelot or Bors,
Or e'en of Galahad, the three we thought
Were sure to make the world ring with their deeds;
And truly, if they fail, not even we
Need strive in further search! Let's stop and rest."
And so they enter'd in an ancient church
That stood near by, and laid their bodies down
Upon the altar-steps, and thus there came
Into their sleep a marvellous dream to each.
First, Gawaine thought he saw into a field
Full strewn with herbs, wherein a rack of bulls
Stood proud and black, save one, all snowy white,
That ever kept its head bent down to graze;
But soon the rest went from the meadow forth,
To seek some pasture-ground they deem'd more rich,
And came back lean and weak, yet would not crop
The fresh, green grass their one wise comrade ate
And strove to lead them to and fully share!
But Ector dream'd that Launcelot and himself
Sprang from one chair upon two saddled steeds;

That one soon met Sir Launcelot on the way,
Who beat and spoil'd him, and then clothed him
o'er
In knotted robes, and set him on an ass;
That thus he rode until he came, athirst,
To a fair well, and stoop'd him down to drink;
But always from his lips the waters sank,
Until at last he sadly journey'd on.
And when the knights awoke, they told their
dreams,
And, as they talk'd, between them sudden rush'd,
Vanishing quick away, a hand that held
A clear light burning, and upon the wrist
A plain, strong bridle hung; and then they rose
To seek some hermit who could meaning give
To these their visions.
Ere they came anigh
To the lone cave where dwelt the holiest man
In all the realm, they met an armèd knight,
Who kept the road, and so they drew a lot
To joust with him to have their pathway clear;
And Gawaine won, and ran his sharp lance through
The stranger's breast, and bore him to the ground.
And when they raised his visor, Ector groan'd;
"For see," he spoke, "thy hasty hand has slain
Our own sworn brother of the Table Round,
That with ourselves set out on this same quest."
"'Tis sad," his comrade said; "but then he stood
So stubborn in our way: besides, his course
Was towards the points we just have left behind;

Thus turn'd, he never could have reach'd the goal!"
And, as his soul departed, they went on.

Then, as they came unto the mountain rough,
They tied their coursers to a rock, and strode
Across the stones afoot, until they reach'd
A garden-patch, wherein a hermit stoop'd
To pick the worts that served for his sole food.
And when he heard the ringing of their mail,
He turn'd his aged form and ask'd their need.
So Gawaine told his dream, and counsel ask'd
Of his great wisdom; and, without more words,
He answer'd thus: "The herbs that strew'd the field
Were Patience and Humility; the rack
Was the Round Table, and the bulls its knights;
The meadow was the world, and that white steer
Was he shall keep himself so pure in life
His eyes shall see the glory of the Lord!
Those black were dyed with sins; and, as their heads
Would stoop not down to taste the precious food,
They shall on waste lands enter, and find death!"
And as Sir Gawaine ponder'd on this speech,
The good seer read Sir Ector's vision too:
"The chair ye left was pride, and, as your steeds
Were higher, ye were so much prouder there.
Sir Launcelot has been cast adown, and clothed
In garments of repentance, and the ass
Betokeneth meekness; but that fair well
Was God's rich grace, that would not touch his soul:
So now he journeys lonely on his way,

Till in due time he shall go back, and quench
His eager thirst within those waters clear.
The hand ye saw was charity; the light
Was hope; the bridle, abstinence, which holds
The heart's desires and leads the will from sin.
And as ye were not touch'd by charity,
Nor long time lit by hope, and have not caught
The reins of passion, and not yet have chew'd
The cud of Patience, ye shall never meet
The Holy Greal until ye win all these.
Now go your ways! Ye neither yet have done
True service to your Maker. As ye gave
To folly all the leaves and fruit of youth,
See that ye yield the bare rind to the Lord."
And then he went from them into his cave;
And both the knights, with eyes bent low, slow paced,
Deep musing, down the stony steep, and loosed
Their restless horses, and rode swift away.

And all the peers that started on the quest
Met strange adventures, and some got sore falls,
Some fainted by the way, and many died.
And some went back to Camelot, and lived
In sloth and ease with lemans fair and false;
But these King Arthur would not see at court,
For, though he grieved at parting with his fréres,
He welcomed none that broke a knightly oath;
Albeit the queen in secret saw them oft,
To ask if e'er they heard of Launcelot aught.

Sir Galahad, the youngest of the knights,
A stranger, and unproved in gallant feats,
Rode by himself four days without a shield:
His heart was tender yet with dreams of youth,
And, as his life was nearer to his birth,
His soul was closer to his God than theirs
Who had forgotten heaven in the heat
Of earthly conflicts mid the light of fame.
He look'd on nature with such earnest love
His rapturous delight to worship soar'd.
His eyes grew gentler as he turn'd aside
His courser's hoofs lest they should heedless tread
To dust and death a daisy in the grass;
And when, unarm'd, he slept in some cool grove
At night beside his weary steed, the stars
Shed down through stirring leaves a sense of peace
Upon a spirit calm'd by trustful prayer.
He knew no fear, because his conscience lay
Like to a lake reflecting cloudless skies:
Not one dark thing o'ershadow'd its bright rest.
And if his mind dwelt oft on that high fate
The seers foretold for him, 'twas with the hope
That his achievements might advance the cause
Of Right and Holiness within the world
He thought so fair, yet knew was foul'd by sin!

Once, after even-song, he came at last
To a white abbey, where he met a knight
Of Arthur's table, who reveal'd to him
That in this place was hung a wondrous shield,

Which none e'er bore in fight and kept unscathed.
"And yet," said Bagdemanus, "I will try,
Because my arm is strong, and sure can keep
By its own skill a shield before my breast!"
So in the morn he took it from its place
Behind the altar, and his comrade saw
'Twas all clear white, save in the midst was limn'd
A shining cross, red as if drawn in blood.
And then he started on adventure forth.
But, ere an hour, in haste his squire came back,
Pale with the tidings that his master lay
O'erthrown near by, and still beset by foes!
And Galahad went out with his bare sword
To where the wounded knight exhausted fell.
He seized the buckler from the feeble grasp,
And straightway was assail'd by countless shapes,
Giants and dwarfs, and bravely stood his ground,
Until at last he felt the storied shield
Slow slipping from his hold, while they who thrust
Their spears against it but the stronger grew
When he look'd faint: so his tried soul cried out
Aloud in anguish for God's gracious help;
And at the sacred Name they sudden sank
From his awed sight away; and then he saw
That a great angel, ray'd about with light,
Upheld his form, who bade him always use
The shield of Faith, since wielded with true Prayer
'Twould keep him ever from attacks of Doubts!

And afterwards, as Galahad went on,

He journey'd in a narrow path o'ergrown
With thorns and briers, where he oft was forced
To cut a way and lead his restless horse,—
Where poisonous vines with noxious smells made
thick
The darken'd air, for branches interlaced
Barr'd light and progress, and from hidden lairs
Glared fiery eyes at him, and stagnant pools
Mock'd eager thirst. Yet still he onward toil'd;
For this, the monks had told him, was the road
Alone could forward him upon his quest.
Sometimes he long'd to throw aside his arms
And rest his weary limbs; but evermore
He saw some work to do, some goal to win
That brought him nearer to the end, nor dared
To slumber, lest he should be stung to death
By creeping creatures, or waste precious hours.
And, as he had such patience for himself,
He felt deep pity for his faithful steed,
And talk'd to him as tenderly as though
It were a woman that was hurt and worn,—
Oft stopping in his labor to smooth down
The ruffled mane, drawing the drooping head
Across his shoulder, and with gentle touch
Stroking the face, until the startled eyes
Grew wistful with a dumb, beseechful love;
And sometimes he would dip his shrinking hand
Into the slimy waters of black tarns,
To wet the bleeding limbs and panting sides.
And so at last they came unto a break

In one side of the road, where grandly stood
A lofty castle with wide-open gates;
And, more because his courser was so maim'd
Than that himself was tempted at the sight,
He enter'd there, and in the outer court
A damsel met, who led his tired steed
To a clean manger stored with straw and food,
The while across his senses faintly fell
Soft breezes of perfume, that wafted by
Delicious melodies, and drew him on
Through the broad portal to a hall, wherein
The only Presence was a leaping fount.
And, as his footsteps waken'd echoes there,
A hidden door flew wide, through which there danced
A troop of mirthful girls, with sandall'd feet,
To cadences of their own mellow strain,
In which their laughter mingled like the tone
Of silvery chorus threading all the tune.
And, as they forward floated where he stood
Entranced an instant by such lustrous eyes,
Their gauzy robes and loosen'd hair flew back,
And white, soft arms uncurved their wreathing grace
To stretch out rosy palms to meet his own;
He felt e'en through the links of his rough mail
The thrills of each light touch, as, group'd around,
They sang a song of greeting that ran thus:—

Enter in from toil and danger!
Ended here thy weary quest!

Now, no more to ease a stranger,
  Thou shalt find reward and rest!
Love the Sancgreal! Love the blest!
  Love's own heaven! it is here!
Hail! all hail! Love's happy guest,
  Welcome here! welcome here!

Love shall fill thy soul with pleasure!
  Love the Sancgreal! Love the dream!
Weaving joys for endless leisure,
  Years will but like moments seem!
Love the Sancgreal! Love the blest!
  Love's own heaven! it is here!
Hail! all hail! Love's happy guest,
  Welcome here! welcome here!

While their bewildering voices fill'd his ear,
Their lithe, fair forms his sight, he, heedless then
Of aught beside, believed their siren words,
And willing follow'd them to fresh surprise.
For, lo! a chamber flooded with a light
Glowing in color without shade or glare,
Wherein were downy couches, spread with stuffs
Of gorgeous dyes deep fringed about with gold,
And poised between rich vases of all flowers
Can thrall the sense with fragrance and bright hues;
And in their midst a table heap'd with fruits
Luscious and ripe, nigh bursting with their juice,
'Mong dainty goblets sparkling with rare wine,
Whose fumes amid the scent of blossoms rose,

Like flames through incense, making warm his
blood.
Athirst and hunger'd, wearied out and worn,
Sir Galahad sat not while women stood,
But lean'd with one arm on the board, while they
Gave ready service to allure his taste:
One brought him clusters of the purple grape,
One pour'd its amber essence, as a third
Stripp'd down the golden orange-rinds,
Or peel'd with jewell'd knife the rosy skin
Of mellow apples; while another broke
The brown stems from crisp, russet pears; he craved
The meat borne in upon its silver dish,
And once his hand crept towards the foaming cups;
But something—either instinct in himself,
Or whisper of an unseen spirit near—
E'er warned him from them all, he knew not why:
So, with cool head and even pulse, he touch'd
No food but simple bread; and as he drain'd
Long draughts of water, while the damsels stared,
One quickly enter'd in their midst, who shone
Among the rest as might the noonday sun
Circled with twinkling stars; and Galahad
Thought for an instant that a minstrel's dream
Had taken shape, to thrill his throbbing heart
With timid wonder that aught out of heaven
Could be so fair. Form, face, voice, movement, dress,
Were all in harmony; and as she stood
Before him, with her vein'd lids droop'd adown,
Giving him welcome in her low, sweet tones,

There rush'd across his soul that one wild wave
Which whelms a proud man's reason, and makes
weak
Earth's strongest Samsons. Suddenly he felt
How lone his life had been, how incomplete,
Half lived, divided as a perfect whole,
Ne'er to be rounded to entireness more
Until his being should absorb and blend
With this one woman's. Love, thus born full-grown,
The spirit's mystic Sancgreal seem'd indeed
That he sought outward sign of!
Days went by
As in a vision; hour in hour roll'd,
Till gliding time like flowing stream swept off
Th' unnoted marks of night and morn that show'd
Its course, and bore his life on rapid waves;
A helmless bark cast loose on unknown depths.
He kept mid luxury his simple ways,
Slept not on downy couches, drank no wine,
Wore still his sword and shield, as though might
come
Some unexpected foe e'en to those halls;
He would not yield to sloth, or fire his blood,
For fear the fallen nature in his flesh
Should sully, e'en in thought, the image pure
He shrined for worship in his inmost soul.
Daily he touch'd her hand, sat at her feet,
Watching the changing beauty of her face;
His jealous envy mark'd when perfumed breeze
Lifted her golden hair; and if he felt

His breath come quick and fast, his youthful blood
Rushing in quicken'd beats, he stole away
To fight his passion till his lips could touch
Her garment's hem as if it were a saint's!
But once, as wearied of such homage high,
She threw aside the long restraint was worn
To win upon his nobleness, and deem'd
Her art had guided him, by slow degrees,
To point of her desire. Athwart his heart
A sharp pain like an arrow shot; a veil
Dropp'd from his charm'd sight; his bright dreams
died!
Gravely and sadly he removed the arms
That clung about him, casting one last look
Of keen reproach upon the angry face,
Then rose and strode away with rapid steps,
Lest he should pause, and turn to love and sin and
shame.
He found his waiting steed, and swiftly rode
Into the narrow way so full of thorns,
Oft hiding mid the briers, holding fast
His courser's mouth, lest he should gladly neigh
When groups of nymphs pass'd by in fruitless search.
He knew the Sancgreal must be farther on,
And took no heed of toil and danger now.
His soul was heavy with its broken trust;
And when he saw the idol he had rear'd
Upon his fancies of pure womanhood
Lie shatter'd by a breath, his sorrow left
His life no other aim save his old quest.

Anon Sir Launcelot, after striving long,
Did see on shore, while sailing on the sea,
A stately castle, and across the waves
A clear voice bade him enter there and find
Some part of his desire. He left the ship;
And, as he near'd the gates, he drew his sword,
Because of two fierce lions station'd close;
But something smote him sore upon the arm,
So that his weapon dropp'd; while the same tone
Accused his little faith, that trusted less
His Maker than his steel; then on his brow
He sign'd the cross, and harmless pass'd the beasts,
That crouch'd in homage. All the doors were wide
Of all the rooms, save one, whence music came;
And, as he vainly tried to stir its lock,
There stole across his soul the same deep sense
Of matchless joy had fill'd his peers that day
They took their oath to seek for it again.
Then on the threshold knelt Sir Launcelot down,
For well he wist the Sancgreal was within,
Praying, if ever he had pleased the Lord,
In spite of all his sins, that he might view
The holy thing he sought! And, lo! the door
Was open'd, and so great a light flow'd out
He scarce could see inside a silver stand,
That held the sacred vessel, cover'd o'er
With crimson samite, and bright angels round,
While hovering over with pierced hands and feet
The very Christ in glory ray'd!

He rose

To seize the Greal; but, ere he came anear,
A breath like burning smote him, that he fell,
And could not move or speak; when unseen hands
Lifted his form and bore him gently out.
He lay entranced for days, till time was ripe,
When other knights of his own fellowship,
Led there from different ways, his body found,
And tended him until his speech return'd;
And then he warn'd them, as they linger'd round
The portal closed they often strove to ope,
Lest they too should be smitten like himself
For over-boldness. "For now I know," he said,
"No man shall win the Sancgreal but the one
Whom Christ shall call! Alas! he call'd not me!"

And so they waited, till Sir Galahad,
After long journeys and adventures strange,
Came in their midst. They wonder'd much to see
His visage greatly changed, for all the youth
And bloom had gone from it, although it show'd
Rare beauty still, as from a grace within;
For he had lived with labor, sorrow, strife,
Yet ever meekly, patiently towards God,
And in true charity with men; his love,
His trial, and his grief, had only borne
His pure soul nigher heaven, and made him see
In other hearts the pain was in his own,
And kept him tender even when he smote.
And when they told him that within those walls
The Sancgreal was, he trembled, and his face

Was rapturous with joy; when, lo! a voice
Call'd three times "Galahad," and the closed door,
Barr'd 'gainst the rest, stood open unto him!
His comrades crowded in the hall, while he,
With timid steps, as doubting his own worth,
Went slowly in, and up the altar-steps,
Where stood the Holy Greal on silver stand.
He bow'd his head before it, as a choir
Of clustering angels sang exquisite strains;
While Christ's own self through circling lustre stretch'd
His wounded hand, when roll'd away the cloth
Of samite, and took up the sacred thing
And gave to him; then in sweet tones, that thrill'd
His listeners, bade him bear it o'er the land,
That all who saw it might be bless'd like him.
And then all vanish'd, save the vessel clasp'd
Close to the young knight's breast, who upward look'd
In praiseful ecstasy, while gather'd round
His peers, to gaze on it with solemn eyes,
And feel how lovely 'twas to draw so near
To aught just come from God; and Galahad
Took oath of them to travel as a guard
For their great gift, that all should help proclaim
Its power and good, that more might know delight.

Then journey'd they in company, save one,
Launcelot, who took the tidings to the king
Or ere he went to tell his own far realm.

And ever on their way the people flock'd
About the marvellous prize; the sick were heal'd,
The blind received their sight, and sinful lives
Grew purer, having known in part the bliss
That reigns in Paradise, and heard it said
Its joy would stay with them who merit proved;
The country's guilt was purged, and hope and love
Walk'd hand in hand, like seraphs, mid its homes!
Till they who humbly should have thank'd the Lord
That He had made them servants of His will,
Quarrell'd between themselves which one had done
The most to make the mighty Sancgreal known;
And at the last, in sooth, they question'd oft
The what it really was!

And Galahad,
Sore smitten, could not stay their angry tilts,
E'en when he went among them with his hands
Outholding the bless'd Greal! And then he pray'd
That Christ would take his spirit to Himself,
Where reign'd His peace. God's mercy heard his cry,
And, in full sight of all His angels, bore
The holy vessel from his dying arms
Up to the highest heaven. And only they
Have ever look'd upon the treasure since
Who pray and fast, and through repentant tears
Catch far-off glimpses of its glory's light.
And while he lay upon his couch and watch'd

The soaring messengers, the knights stood round,
E'en mid their mourning, all disputing still,
And asked him, ere he pass'd away, to tell
What he had deem'd the Sancgreal really was!
And Galahad uplifted his weak form,
And with his white face awed them, as his lips,
Quivering with death, spoke out his last, grand
words:
"O Men! 'twas Truth! God's own Eternal Truth!"

THE LAST MEETING OF LAUNCELOT AND GUINEVERE.

Over the sea, from Castle Joyous Garde,
Once more to England came Sir Launcelot back,
Hearing King Arthur was so sore beset
By traitor Mordred, who had dared to lift
His wistful eyes towards the peerless queen,
And with his treacherous sword to shake the throne,
As once his troublous tongue had stirr'd the heart—
The grand, large heart—of him who sat thereon,
By whispering of the love she bore to Launcelot!
But when with seven kings he landed there,
The people told him of the battle past,
And how that Arthur died that fearful day.
"Ah, woe is me! I would a man might weep!"
The brave knight said, and clutch'd his broad shield
close;

"For ne'er to me such heavy tidings came!
Fair lords, I thank ye all for your good will
That bore ye with me to this country here,
Wherein we came too late, for both are kill'd,—
The princely gentleman we came to save,
The damnéd traitor that we came to slay!
My life will not be long enough to grieve
In sore repentance for our lacking speed;
But 'gainst the death that robb'd my vengeful steel
No man may dare rebel! And, sith 'tis so,
I ride myself to seek my ladye-queen,
Who, sick and sad, has fled towards the west;
I go alone; nay, when knew Launcelot fear?
And if for me the realm be perilous
That once was my dear home, I wear my sword,
And still can lift an arm'd man from the ground.
Await ye here for just a fortnight's space;
And if I come not then, take all your ships
And go again to your own lands; for I
Will do as I have told you heretofore.
Farewell, kind comrades! tried, true friends, adieu!"

So Launcelot unto Almesbury came,
Not knowing Guinevere abided there,
And rested him in prayer before the shrine;
Then, as he walk'd adown the cloister'd aisle,
Sudden he met the queen, all white and weak,
For she had seen him doff his casque and kneel,
And swoon'd three times or ere she trembling rose,

And bade the nuns stand far the while she went
And talk'd with her old love once more.
He bow'd,
Pallid as she; for all his heart leap'd up
With one quick, passionate throb to greet
The woman whom he loved; and yet respect
For her great grief, her sacred garb, controll'd
To knightly homage his first eager thrill.
His strong arms yearn'd to fold her to his breast,
His parching lips to kiss that quivering mouth
Into the crimson of its former smile,
Or close those heavy lids with fond caress;
He was athirst to see that precious face,
So wan and changed, yet dearer for the change,
Upturn'd to his with one sweet look of yore!
But, check'd, subdued by those sad eyes, that robe,
He stoop'd with courtly mien to touch her hand.
She held it back beneath her coarse serge sleeve,—
The little hand that used to meet his own,
Palm close to palm, in such delicious clasp,
In those old times at Camelot, when he wore
Her silken scarf at tournament or joust!
Something that seem'd a tear flash'd o'er his sight!
Was it a dream that she had loved him once?
Was it a dream when the soft voice, kept cold
By her stern will, bade him return again
To his own land, that nevermore her soul
Might be in peril from her sight of him?
Was it a dream that she accused their love
Of all the evils that the kingdom mourn'd,

And, sighing, told "her life was vowed to prayer"?
He listen'd as if one of Merlin's spells
Had bound his sense in silence, till she said,
Her hand upon her heart, "That he should wed;
That he would soon forget, in his fair realm,
A fading queen reft of her grace and state;
Or if sometimes, when, for a little space,
He thought of her and all their guilty past,
He but would pray God's peace on her the while
He had grown happy with a gentle wife,
She thought that she might die without regret!
And if—oh, if——"

Here sobs broke up her speech,
And Launcelot knelt as one that takes an oath,
While she, half bending, dropp'd upon his brow
Hot tears, that stirr'd his manhood into words!
"My heart's one love! thou knowest ne'er on earth
Shall other love than thine be aught to me!
O Guinevere, hast thou forgot how oft
I promised thee I would be always leal?
Was Launcelot ever false unto his vows?
I am as true as when I told my love,
And thou didst come into my waiting arms,
Blushing and trembling with life's perfect bliss!
Ah, no,—my queen,—no wife for me,—no land,
No hope in this world left! I, too, will give
My coming days to prayer; wilt thou, too, pray
That we may meet again beyond the grave?
My love will live e'en there,—O Guinevere!
My love! my own, own love!"

And here he stoop'd
And kiss'd her sandall'd foot. With one great cry,
One look to heaven, she turn'd to flee from him;
And he fell prostrate, moaning with despair!
For one long minute, like an age of strife,
She battled with the wild, wild wish to lift
His head upon her bosom as of yore,—
To live again, e'en though 'twas deadly sin,
One hour of love, and then—then die of joy!
She almost knelt to touch his clustering hair,
Her pale cheek flush'd, her panting breath came
fast,—
When, like the voice of God, the vesper-hymn
Gave her weak woman's heart to angels' charge.
Their love,—the present,—her youth's lover there,—
Seem'd to grow dim before the cross of Christ;
Her agony was o'er; the thorns upon her brow
Became a crown of light through passion slain!
She found the Sancgreal in that trial-hour!
A vision of unspoken glory fill'd
Her raptured view, and, when it died away,
It left her face as 'twere the face of one
Who might have talk'd with God!
And Launcelot rose,
And look'd upon her countenance, and knew
He was no more to her!
And yet he craved,
Ere he should go from her for evermore,
That he might kiss her once, but only once,
For sake of their old love and his long truth!

She waved her hand, as when upon the throne
She would dismiss a minstrel or a squire;
Nor did he dare to ask again the boon
He long'd to take: "her life was vowed to heaven!"
But, fading slowly through the twilight dim,
Pass'd from her sight into the outer world;
And mid the stillness sang the solemn choir,
"*Kyrie Eleison! Christe, exaudi nos!*"

LAUNCELOT'S VIGIL.

Launcelot du Lake, that had been bravest knight,
Launcelot du Lake, whom Guinevere had loved,
Launcelot du Lake, whom all the world had praised,
For very sorrow threw aside his sword,
And folded o'er his slowly-breaking heart
A monk's coarse robe, and in a narrow cell
Forgot the world, and learn'd to serve his God!
And thither came to him, to share alike
Penance and fasting, seven other lords,
Whose armor rusted in the chapel vaults
The while they pray'd together at the shrine,—
His old-time friends, that in the storied days
Had with each other jousted, jested, rode,
And pledged their ladies' names at merry feasts,
And lived the thoughtless life that scars the soul.

Launcelot the monk, changed from the gallant sir
That never met his peer in field or hall,
Slumber'd, and saw a vision as he slept,—
Saw once again, amid the dreams of night,
The woman's face that was his earthly fate,—
The queen's,—but not as she had used to come
Into his sleeping thoughts that brought so oft
Her tender tones, her clinging kiss, her eyes
Looking in his with love's fond, rapturous gaze,
But as a man whose deep, repentant zeal
Has scourged the flesh, till passion, pride of life,
And all base things are banish'd from the soul
That sees, through pain, the glory of the Lord;
Or with the spirit, freed from mortal taint,
With other spirits holds communion strange.
She bent above his worn and pallid cheek,
That flush'd not now to feel her mouth so near,
And mid the solemn silence call'd his name,
And bade him unto Almesbury haste,
To find her dead; from thence to bear her forth
And bury her beside her husband, the great king,
Who would forgive her when she came once more
To rest beside him on his royal couch;
For prayer and penitence had purged her life
From her youth's sin, and she could meet him now!

So Launcelot rose ere it was day, and went,—
The seven others with him,—went once more
Journeying together in the open air,
Feeble and weak who once were stout and strong,

And smiled not as of yore to see afar
The spires of Camelot glitter in the sun.
And when they enter'd at the nunnery gate,
The ladies told them that the queen was dead,
And murmur'd, ere her voice was hush'd in death,
That Launcelot thither came to read her mass.
And as they talk'd, his hot tears fell adown,
And faltering words ask'd if aught else she spake;
And gentle hearts held back unwelcome truth,
Until he urged the answer:—"That she pray'd,
Till her last breath, that nevermore her eyes
With living sight might see Sir Launcelot's form!"
And Launcelot turn'd his face towards the wall,
That those near by should mark not in his look
Of mortal agony the sudden throe.

They laid her in the broad aisle of the church,
Before the altar, and lit all the lights;
And o'er the bier, instead of sable pall,
They cast the purple cloak she wore that day
She fled from throne and strife for shelter there.
And Launcelot kept the midnight watch alone—
The last—with her,—with Guinevere,—the dead!
He sang her dirge who erst had whisper'd words
Into those willing ears had thrill'd her heart,—
That heart whose throbbing pulses then had leap'd
In burning blushes when he came anear,
And stirr'd the very velvet that now lay
So still upon the silent shape; the while
He breathed her name, her dear name, in such tones

As might have reach'd her in the deepest grave!
He read her mass, and wept between the prayers,
Imploring God, for Christ's incarnate sake,
To give her peace, to take her to His rest,
That so, when Arthur met her as she walk'd
White-robed, with angels, in the golden street,
He might forget her human sin, and know
That God's forgiveness seal'd her his true wife!

And, when his sacred duty was all done,
He rose from kneeling 'neath the host, and look'd
Once more upon her face,—and then—and then
His full heart broke! He thought of all the past;
He saw her, as at first, a fair, young bride,
Regal, yet shy of state, and glad to be
Apart from court, and laughing with her maids,
Or riding 'neath green boughs with loosen'd hair,
Or dancing changing measure with rare grace.
He felt again the thrill that fired his blood
When first her soft palm, trembling, press'd his own;
He saw the drooping lash, the dewy mouth
Waiting his proud caress in other times,
And lived again each hour of passionate joy,
Sweeter for being secret, save that now
Each left upon his soul the weight of crime!
He bow'd to kiss her lips,—to clasp again
Those marble hands. A sort of fierce delight
Flash'd through his frame to think that his should be

The last warm touch should ever linger there!
Ah, no! ah, no! he dared not! She had gone
To be forgiven: it was not meet that she
Should bear in Eden seal of former shame.
She had o'erlived her love: he had no right
Even to look upon her with the olden thoughts,
Since that was lost had sanctified their guilt!
Renunciation was his office's oath!
It was God's justice he should suffer this!
And she slept there, so cold, so pale, so still,—
And he stood by, so shaken with his grief,
Memories, remorse, all passions that can war
In a man's mind,—and over both the cross.
He deem'd if he had seen her only once,
Once more before she died, and heard her say
His love was pardon'd, and the ill it wrought,—
If her last sigh had only pass'd away
Upon his breast,—he could have borne to know
That he must live without her in the world!
But she had plead to see him nevermore!
Was it, perchance, because she fear'd to feel
The old dream wake again in her last hours?
He quiver'd with the hope, and eager sought
To catch upon the stony brow one trace
Of the dear look that thrall'd him in his youth.
Not there!—not there!—she loved her husband now,
And in the sight of God she gazed on him
With those sweet eyes, all purified by death!
And Launcelot paced the lonely aisles, and fought
With his own soul until he tamed his woe,

And went not mad with anguish that long night!
Then, just at dawn, he knelt beside the corpse,
And pray'd that, if so be he yet should win
A place in paradise, it might be where,
In Christ's wide heaven, she ne'er might see his face!
For, as he cast such sorrow on her life,
He would not shadow her immortal bliss
Even by memories he would cherish still
Through all eternity apart from her!

And the next day they laid her in the earth
Beside the king, and in the open tomb
Sir Launcelot saw them lying side by side,
And swoon'd to think that he had loved her so,
And yet should be so far away from her
When at the resurrection-morn they two
To the last judgment would together rise!
So, day by day, he came unto the grave,
And mourn'd and faded, till his strength no more
Could bear him from his couch, and then he died,—
Died with a smile upon his lips, like one
Who takes into his dreams a lingering kiss!

And all his seven fréres had sworn to him
That they would bury him at Joyous Garde;
And, as he lay in state in his own land,
With the queen's scarf cross'd on his shrunken breast,
That he so oft at tournaments had worn,

Sir Ector spoke his requiem with tears:-
"Lie there, Sir Launcelot, head of Christian knights!
That never yet was match'd by earthly peer,
The courtliest lord that ever bore a shield,
The noblest friend that ever shared the salt,
The truest lover ever couch'd a spear!
Thou wert the gallantest that ever rode,—
The goodliest person in the press of knights,—
The kindest man to ladies in the hall,
The sternest to thy mortal foe in field!
Lie there, Sir Launcelot, and in future days,
When men shall seek example for their sons,
They shall but say, 'Be brave as Launcelot was,—
Launcelot, who was the bravest, gentlest knight
In all King Arthur's court,—in all the world!
Flower of chivalry, servant of his God!'"

AVILION.

> "The island valley of Avilion,
> Where falls not hail, nor rain, nor any snow,
> Nor ever wind blows loudly; but it lies
> Deep-meadow'd, happy, fair with orchard lawns
> And bowery hollows crown'd with summer sea!"
>
> *Tennyson's "Morte d'Arthur."*

"Arthur should come again!" the prophet said
The kingdom waited long, and each great soul
That star-like rose upon the nation's sky

Was watch'd for token of expected fate
That should achieve the change and good desired.
But never one fulfill'd the perfect dream
Of stainless character and lofty aim
That in tradition lived and hoping minds.
And, reading this, I murmur'd to myself,
"'Tis better so: the people must be great
That keep such standard of high excellence
Their best do never reach! So let me use
The gift the fairies gave me at my birth
To set in common view, with Saxon words,
A living image of the ideal knight,
Lest men forget, amid these restless times
Of hollow shows and worshipping of gold,
That truth and pureness once were in the world,
Nor lose their faith that they will come again!
And so I sang the songs of other days,—
Have ta'en to modern homes and modern hearts
The ghosts of ancient dead that lived their lives
As grandly or as weakly as their age
Or natures wrought on them! with my witch-wand
I open'd Fancy's portal, and led forth
In their own shapes, to breathe earth's air again,
The storied men who had become a name,
And group'd them all about the British king,
As once they circled him at Table Round,
And that fair queen, so frail because she loved,
That, false herself, kept her one lover true,
Whom Arthur trusted, blind to his great wrong,

Since his large, royal soul in others saw
Only the good and truth was in his own.

And then I said, with that vague, quenchless thirst
We dreamers know when mingles sorrow's shade
With discontent at our own labor done,
That seems so poor beside the vivid thought,
"And what reward is mine for this my work?
Men will forget it in a little while,
And when this brain is dust, how few will care
That once it throbb'd with Inspiration's heat!
Would I could go away from all the doubt,
The pain and turmoil of this weary life,
Into Avilion, where the good king went,
And rest me in the Happy Isle, like him!"
And so I closed my tired eyes, that press'd
Two tears between the lids, that, as they touch'd
The level ground, into a wonder grew;
For, lo! a lake that spread its waters up
Nigh to my feet, while through the sunset glow
A black barge hove in sight, like one that came
For wounded Arthur, only now it bore
No fair, crown'd queens, no hooded, weeping dames!
Only a pallid steersman stood at helm,
With white garb stirless as a statue's robe,
That seem'd to sweep adown o'er folded wings.
The boat came slowly to the coast, and paused.
I inland turn'd an instant's sight, and saw
That darkness gather'd o'er the fields, and light
Was all before, then stepp'd into the stern,

And o'er the rising tide the vessel moved.
We floated on; my comrade never spoke,
And I sat silent, with a lonely sense
Born from the far-off look in his sad eyes.
But once, remembering Charon, I arose
And laid a coin within his idle hand;
He gazed at it in wonder, curved his arm,
And dropp'd it in the waves; and, half abash'd,
I turn'd towards the glories of the sky.
The slanting rays shot up the azure arch
In silver streaks that waned in motes away,
Tinging the fleecy clouds with rainbow hues;
We sail'd on golden ripples, whose light foam
Died on th' horizon's verge, where, half in heaven,
A purple island hung with rosy shores;
While stretching off on either side there shone
White lustrous mountains edged with peaks of fire.
We came anear at last. Delicious airs
Play'd o'er my brow, that brought a faint, rare sound
Of distant harmony; while through my limbs
New vigor ran, that sent the dancing blood
Tingling in languid veins, as each heart-throb
More quick and eager with expectance grew.
In buoyant feelings I had long forgot,
My youth and hope came back to me once more;
And, like the slow uprising of a mist,
There roll'd away the darkness that was laid
Between my mind and things I strove to solve;
Deep, secret meanings dawn'd upon my brain,

That had been dull'd with dust, but in this clime
Saw clear the hidden truth. Sorrow and pain,
That woke such wild, blind prayers, look'd only
now
As ministers to purify desire;
And e'en the earth's great riddle that we beat
Rebellious wills 'gainst,—ah! I may not show
What grand significance e'en evil took!
And, as I leap'd upon the shining beach,
I cried, "How few in that old world of woe
E'er dream'd the Happy Island lay so near!"
And such rich rapture stirr'd my grateful soul,
I bent my knee in worship's ecstasy,
Thanking my God that, after years of toil
To know the Truth, and fallings by the way,
My Faith in Him had stood the test of Thought!
But most my spirit thank'd Him that He is!
And, as I rose, one that I knew stood by,
And look'd in mine with eyes as tender, soft
As when we parted—ah! so long ago!
"I knew that you would come!" he said, when first
The bliss of meeting yielded feeling words;
"And I have waited here; for all the joys
Of this fair home were incomplete and poor
Till I had you once more, my life's beloved!
See these green lawns, these shaded, quiet woods,
Where we will walk together, as of yore,
And never change or part, or weep or yearn!
Was it not worth the tears we shed on earth
To love forever in Avilion thus?"

And so we talk'd a while, until I ask'd,
"I marvel that 'tis light here still! 'twas dusk
Beyond there when I started! Does the sun
Ne'er set on this bless'd land?" He gently said,
"At eventime there shall be light!" and then
I knew no night would e'er dispel the glow
That rested on this isle from unseen source.
And afterwards I question'd of the prince,
If yet he dwelt here while the nations wait;
And my dear comrade took my willing hand,
And led me through the shadowy lanes, wherein
He said we might meet Arthur and the queen.

I think mine eyes had glimpses of the views,
Through opening glades, that once my dreams be-
lieved
Were parts of all fair countries far away
That I had never seen,—green slopes and swells,
And high hills veil'd in floating, silver mists,
And countless waterfalls, and limpid streams
Where trees droop'd o'er and shaded lotus buds;
And 'neath our feet and all about us bloom'd
Rich, unknown blossoms, and the twining leaves
A dewy freshness bore; and in the midst
I walk'd in silent rapture, such as comes
To human hearts in love's divinest hour,
When speechless bliss o'erfloods the tender gaze
And lifts th' aspiring soul through joy to God!
And there was nothing of the sadness here
That stole through all the Nature I had known,

And made it ever seem like some vain show
In which a spirit grieves; but flowers and sky,
Meadow and stream, were freely, fully bright,
As if the soul of happiness inspired
Their life and beauty, where no sorrow came;
And all the higher pleasures of mere sense
Were so etherealized, we could but feel
A fine expansion, taintless of all flesh!
And, as we walk'd together as of yore,
Slow pacing mid the avenues of trees,
Then through an arching vista I beheld
A street of gold that ran 'twixt crystal domes,
And two that came adown its sparkling slope;
And, as we drew anear, I saw that one
Was grand in presence, kingly, and yet wore
Such courteous, kindly mien, that one who begg'd
Might call him "brother," though he graced a throne!
And clinging to his arm, with white hands link'd,
And small head thrown aback with all its wealth
Of flowing hair, that thus the loving eyes
Might seek the lofty face, was one that seem'd
The very fairest creature e'er I saw.
"Ah! see! they come!" my dear companion said,
"The king and Guinevere!" and, as he ceased,
We met them face to face, and Arthur spake
To one he knew a stranger, in sweet tones
Of simple welcome; and then, mid our talk,
He ask'd, at last, "Do those you left behind
Still keep a thought of me? Do men still hope

That I will come again, as Merlin told,
To do my best to win for them the right?"
And when I drew a picture of the times,
And how the nations groan'd because was found
No strong, true leader pure in life and aim,
He turn'd aside, as if to muse alone;
And one came slowly up between the glades,
On whose worn face there shone a holy smile,
That might have been a seraph's, and stood by
The while the queen ask'd, with a watchful glance
Towards the prince, "Do men on earth still love
As in the olden time? Do ladies keep
Their faith the same in spite of keen despair.?"
I answer'd not, but fondly clasp'd the hand
That touch'd mine own, and something in our looks
Spoke more than words unto her woman-sense.
"Ah, well!" she said, without a sigh, or shade
On her smooth brow, "we too loved well as you
In years that are a dream, Isonde and I!
But then we loved with wrong, and pray'd to God,
Long ere we died, to wipe our deep sin out;
And when we came here, all our feelings clung
Whereto they ought, ere led astray by flesh!
See, now I stand by Launcelot, and no thrill
Stirs him or me: I love my lord the king!"
And I, remembering oft-repeated tales
Of their great passion, then towards Launcelot turn'd,
A sudden pity quivering on my mouth;
But he, with glowing brow and shining eyes,

Look'd up as if a vision met his view,
And murmur'd softly, through his parted lips,
"My God! my God! I love but Thee, my God!"
And just then Arthur came to me, and spoke
Like one whose mind has measured some resolve
And master'd it: "The time at last is ripe!
I will go back again! The people need
A chief whose soul knows glories that will lift
His deeds and motives o'er all petty price.
I wore a crown before, and felt its thorns;
And I have known since what it is to live
In heavens won by duty: so I go
To lead the way to truth through seas of blood!
Come with me, while I sit me down once more
Among the knights that shared my Table Round;
For who may tell if I can keep myself
Unscath'd by sin, and here return again?
My own dear queen! I never thought to see
A tear in sweet Avilion! Pray to God,
Who sends me on His errand, that His love
Shall compass me about until the end;
'Twill not be long to wait: you know, beloved,
A thousand years in His sight are a day!"

And so we went together to a vale
Bosom'd in verdant hills, where waters lay,
And round about, upon the lilied lawns,
A goodly company of noble men.
And Arthur sat him on a rising knoll,
With Guinevere's bow'd head upon his breast,

And told his high resolve, and ask'd of each
Some counsel of their wisdom, that his soul
Might carry back into the lives of men
The teachings won through death by heavenly thought.
And as they throng'd about him with deep words,
And deeper meanings, answering to his need
With wondrous axioms that each one had wrung
The pith of from a sharp experience,
I soon was 'ware that, mid the knightly shades
That once for right clash'd swords at Camelot,
Came large-brow'd, lifted heads, light-crown'd like kings;
And these with tuneful voices utter'd slow
Such music, knowledge, and prophetic sense,
I scarce knew which most marvellous seem'd to hear,
So blended with a simple, quiet ease
Was tone melodious and thought sublime.
And in a pause my comrade softly said,
"These are the poets, dear: before, we knew
Their minds by flashes; but from their own lips,
Oft wandering by these everlasting streams,
We now shall share the fulness of their growth,
And hear old strains completed that were left
With something wanting in our other sphere!"

The poets! O my poets! how I long'd
To see your faces once! How your sweet words
Have stirr'd the pulses of my hot young heart

Or still'd its fever! Masters, singers, skalds!
Ye were my friends that never play'd me false,
The teachers ever pointing to the True!
Your names lie gather'd in my inmost soul,
As cherish'd as the flowers that we keep
In token of great happiness and love!
O souls inspired, through whom amid my woe
I stretch'd my hands to God! I look'd on you,
Saw your grand foreheads, heard your voices clear,
And could not tell, for gazing in your eyes,
If white shapes hovering round your steps were they
Whose names your songs made glorious for aye,
The women ye had loved, or angels charm'd
From other heavens by the music here.
I saw ye all, my bards! ay, mine and earth's,
God's and eternity's! Albeit I saw
Where thorns had pierced your brows, and naked feet
Were scarr'd from treading ploughshares red with pain!

My stately Sophocles with Shakspeare walk'd,
Two royal natures mated, with a space
Betwixt their purple and the next who came;
Yet they were men too grand to look on men,
And blinded that they should but see the gods!
One sang to Grecian harp the world's child-faith,
And one its manhood's to a loftier lyre!
Homer and Milton, with majestic eyes,

That saw us tremble at their awful runes!
Then Sappho, with her hand in Tasso's twined,
Her fruitless passion spent in that wild leap
When flashing of her robe the ages thrill'd!
And he sublime through sorrow born of love,
Without a speck of prison-dust to float
'Twixt his fond hope and glories of his dream!
And crush'd Italia's boast, that sets her high
Above the thrones that cannot seize at least
Her great crown-gems, outshining all their power!
Virgil and Dante, with the sadness fled
Their human brows once caught among the lost!
Then Spenser, Chaucer, that had lived so near
To Nature's heart, they show'd us how our own
Throbb'd pulse to pulse with hers! While two grand forms
Came, with a prince between, who loved them well,
And made himself a prouder tomb than his
Of the same name who slept enthroned at Aix!
For, dropping out the sceptre from his hand,
He laid him down at last betwixt the dust
That bore eternal fames, and link'd his grave
On either side to sacred soil for aye!
The rare completed man of many lives,
Whose eager search strove ever towards the truth,
And sang the gleams he caught in deathless notes,
Great Goethe show'd in meanings of his speech
That earth's unquiet quest was found at last!
And that fine nature, brother of his mind,
True lover of the beautiful and free,

Schiller, who trod the highest paths of Art,
With Carl of Weimar looking upon both
As Saul might once have gazed upon the seer
That pour'd anointing oil upon his head!
Byron and Burns, those passionate, rich souls,
That here, unfetter'd from all scorn and ill
And weakness of the flesh, had grown sublime
By living purely out their higher selves;
Inspired of genius still, whose burning words
Startled a glance of fire to Arthur's eyes,
That faded into awe as solemn rose
The voice of one amid the moment's hush
That might have been a prophet of the Lord
To shake and gather spirits in the world,
If time and reason could have cast from life
The hot dreams of his youth ere death had led
His seeing mind unto the Fount of Light!
And after Shelley, with his trembling lips
Uttering low music into language breathed,
Endymion pass'd, who left to mark his rest
The record of a name in water writ,
And found his high thoughts known beyond the stars!
And as they moved aside, they group'd around
A fair, slight form but late come in their midst,
That stood within the circle of their tones
Calmly as one who long had known each soul,
Yet with a gladness shining on her face
Like to an exile's who is welcomed home
By old familiar voices, answering all

With some remember'd token of the past!
The mighty ancients spoke to her in words
As musical as choruses they sung;
The soul-blind minstrels of dim, distant days
Stood side by side with martyrs who had mix'd
The last triumphant strains of holy lives
With hatred's incense of ascending flames;
And all sublime and tender hearts that loved
And gave love language in their native tongues
That won new harmony from notes divine;
And they who play'd on lutes by sorrow tuned,
Or lifted nations, in a burst of song,
From deep despair to heights of conquering faith,—
These talk'd with her as one whom their blest sight
Saw worthy evermore to walk with them
In amaranthine fields 'neath trees that bear
The leaves of knowledge and the fruit of life!
And some there were that breathed in broken sounds
Such thrilling, earnest thoughts, I could but feel
That they had been the voiceless ones of earth,
Trying their new-won power with timid lips,
As children stammer ere they learn to speak!
Yet, as all cluster'd round the central shape,
As in the skies the constellations range
About a single star, ofttimes less bright
And smaller than the suns that orbit it,
She spoke some reverent word that drew reply,
Pointing her hands towards the far-off world,

Then towards the glowing beams of changeless
light
Wherein the good king sat among his knights;
And all the streams and woods, and hills and vales,
Gave solemn echo to the glad refrain,
Suiting all time when wrong by right is slain,
Of "Pan, Great Pan is dead! Pan, Pan is dead!"

And, as the last note floated low away,
Arthur arose, and shoreward turn'd his steps,
And all the company went with him there;
Launcelot and Galahad on either side
Walk'd, with their lustrous faces, though one show'd
That pureness had belong'd to it from birth,
And to the other came through pain and death;
Then Bors and Bedivere, Sir Gareth, Kaye,
Tristan and Pellinore, Gawaine and Urre,
And all the other proud, familiar names
That shook the lists with shoutings in old days.
And the fair queen, after quick rain of tears,
With head uplifted like to one who sees
The bow of promise, all the storm forgot
In listening to the music of the bards.
And when we came upon the sparkling beach,
The barge was waiting, but the helmsman now
Was a great seraph, crown'd, with wings outspread,
Whose glory circled him as rays the sun.
And Arthur enter'd in, and round his form
The angel's radiance made wondrous light.
And some would fain have shared with him again

This new adventure ; but he simply said,
" 'Twas written I should go alone! my work
Needs not that more be banish'd from their heaven!
Nay, nay, dear friends! It is the will of God!"
And at the sacred Name all bow'd their heads
And let him pass, and, as the vessel heaved
On waves of golden light, the air seem'd full
Of glorious faces and of snowy plumes,
And over us unnumber'd voices join'd
In such sweet harmony, it swell'd the tears
In speechless ecstasy from my touch'd heart.
And then—and then—was it the stirring sail
Or sudden silence broke the marvellous spell?
Alas! I know not! only, in a flash,
I found myself once more within this world,
On which the shades had gather'd into night,
And mid the throng that wait the Coming King!

MARBLE ISLE.

MARBLE ISLE.

A SHIP went forth from merrie England's shore,
A stately ship, with sunlight on the sails,
Freighted by hopes and wafted on by prayers,—
Went forth to float in distant unknown seas,
To rest in lonely ports, where ne'er before
Came English voice to stir the silent air.
Mothers had bless'd their boys, and sires their sons,
Sisters had sobb'd farewell, and dearer hearts
Had broken in their wordlessness of grief
When all their world pass'd from their straining sight;
Each parting kiss, each fond, last yearning look,
Had crush'd brave manhood's boasted pride of mien,
And woke the fount of tears in woman's soul;
And hands had met with tighter strength of grasp
To force the tear-drops from too willing eyes
Back on the o'ercharged heart, to gush again
In faster flow when freed from long restraint,
Until the weepers smiled in very scorn
To feel themselves grow weaken'd by their woe;
And there were broken accents and low tones,

And quivering lips below hard, firm-knit brows,
Fond, hurried promises, and sad replies,
And oft-repeated names, that grew more dear
To those that bore them for each loving look
And tender lingering o'er the precious sound.
Then sudden sunderings of clasping arms,
The swiftly hoisted flag unfurling slow,
A stir, a shout re-echoed from the land,
A booming shot that drown'd each parting shriek,—
And all was o'er: a ship had gone to sea!
The land was green as each one look'd farewell;
The breeze was odorous with new-mown hay;
The ripen'd grain waved golden in the sun;
While rippling meadows sparkled with their dew,
Like emerald lakes that bore a fleet of flowers;
Each hawthorn hedge was musical with song;
The fruit-trees bow'd beneath their weight of wealth,
And children gather'd acorns in the woods.
The land was green. Long after, they who sail'd
Look'd longing back upon the home they left,
And loved it more that it was fresh and fair;
And, as they last beheld it, memory kept
Its picture thus: their native land was green!

A ship went out to sea, sail'd full of souls,—
Went forth, but back again came nevermore!
Mothers grew pale with watching, wept, and died;
And fathers went about their daily work
With slower step, oft stopping by the way

To muse in silence, sighing towards the sea,
Or, starting, fancy that a shadow swept
Across their path in likeness of their son,
The while dark locks turn'd white, and creeping
years
But made them cling more closely in their age
To one, the absent, than all other ties;
And sisters still remember'd in their prayers,
Morning and night, the wandering sailor's name,
Or, as time sped apace, hush'd baby cries
With promises of rare and wondrous things
Their unknown kinsman, if he ever came,
Would bring from distant lands beyond the main;
While of the dearer hearts, some never ceased
To keep alive Hope's flame till quench'd by Death,
Cheating suspense with some delusive dream,
Or, fading slow with fear, were faithful still,
To meet reward at last, when those they loved
Gave watcher's welcome on th' eternal shore;
And some wore weeds a while, then heard again
Love's wooing words, and found another mate,
Losing mid newer cares youth's parting pang;
Children were born to them, rear'd up, and sent
On separate paths to find their future fate;
And it may be, some younger, daring soul
Turn'd seaward, and recall'd her girlhood's grief
In anxious weeping for the Outward Bound!
And there were tears to shed o'er little graves,
Tears for some footstep that would rove astray,
Some erring one to whom the mother-heart

Clung ever closer as it farther stray'd;
Tears forced by poverty, by loss, by pain,
Uncounted tears for countless passing ills,
Sorrows that spread, like thickest mourning-veil
Between the present and their life's past woe.
And some lived long, and, seated by the fire
In arm-chair shelter'd in the warmest nook,
Their children's children climb'd their willing knee,
Coaxing their grand-dame with their lisping lips
For fairy legend, tale of olden time,
Or, best of all, that history of her youth
Of how she travell'd to a far-off town
And saw a stately ship go out to sea
That never, never more came back again;
Nor noted, in their eager, listening mood,
How the old voice was sweeter, low, and sad,
Whene'er she spoke of one who sail'd that morn,—
Although she told the story as she felt,
So long ago the time and scene had been,
As if the blooming girl left lone that day
Was not herself, but some one she had known.
Nor could they deem how through a weary life,
While hair, and hope, and all things else wax'd gray,
That touch of memory kept her heart still green.

And there was one, a woman young and fair,
Who came that morn to bid her love farewell,
Whom she had wounded with the passing scorn
Of thoughtless girlhood in her pride of power,
Then pined in wonder that he came no more,
Until a message bade her meet him there,

That, pardoning, he might pray her to forgive
The hasty act that banish'd him from her.
And so she came. The ship had sail'd an hour,
Holding one bitter heart amidst its crew,
With lips that no last kiss kept pure from sin.
And she! the hidden feelings of long days,
The speechless anguish of repentant nights,
The desolation of her woman's life,
Swept up in one great wave of swelling woe
Upon her heart, as 'gainst th' horizon's verge
Dash'd sapphire billows into deeper depths!
She could not die; for he was yet alive!
So, moaning in her pride of lonely grief,
She turn'd aside to seek a place to weep,
And found it in a gray-hair'd seaman's arms,—
An old, rough man, who took her to his breast
Like a hurt child, and soothed with rude, kind words,
As if the golden head he shelter'd so
Awoke some memory of his far-off youth,
Until the vessel that his bosom bore,
The tattoo'd token of a distant voyage,
Heaved on the brine that wet its aged keel,
And the scarr'd hand swept o'er the dim, worn eyes,
That, unrestrain'd at last, shared tears with hers.—
And when th' allotted time had lapsed away,
And anxious hearts had said the ship was due,
They came again, the old man and the girl,
Daily, for months, in sunshine and in storm,
To sit together on a jutting crag

And look across those ever-rolling waves;
While harden'd men grew gentle at the sight,
And sternest voices whisper'd words of hope,
Till Pity dared not bid her longer dream;
And then they silent stood whene'er she pass'd,
Bowing before her sorrow with wet eyes.
And when she came no more, they call'd the rock,
Whereon her life had wasted slow away,
"The Watcher's Wait;" and so they name it yet.
Each morn they came, he patient with her woe,
And she half fever'd with her fadeless trust
That each new day would bless her yearning eyes.
And thus, with lips apart and tight-clasp'd hands,
She watch'd each sail that whiten'd o'er the blue,
Upstarting, if it homeward near'd the port,
To seek with longing gaze for one dear form,
Or drooping 'neath sharp disappointment's sting,
As, speeding onward, it escaped her view.
And sometimes, half unconscious that she wept,
Great tears would drop and mingle with the waves
O'er which she lean'd, upbraiding with her pain;
And as they fell, the mariner would think,
"Perchance in some old sea-cave where he lies,
Borne mid yon waters, they may touch the lips
She ne'er will press again!" And then he grew
More careful and more tender of his charge;
And when the twilight shadow'd o'er the sea,
He led her home, still turning as she went,—
Until, one day, when from the stormy clouds
The sun burst sudden out, till all the foam,
White-cresting angry deeps that fought the winds,

Flash'd with the glory of a victor's crown,
All sparkling diamonds on an emerald helm;
There, as she sat upon the bare, brown rock,
With long hair loose and heavy with the rain,
Her pale face leaning 'gainst her comrade's arm,
Slowly there came a change upon her look,
A gathering meaning, as the Northern seer's
When first his vision marks some phantom-shape,
Then, lifting up her head, gazed o'er the sea,
Transfix'd and silent, like to one who sees
A Gorgon shield; then brightly, like that burst
Of sudden sunlight, shone a happy smile,
Chasing all gloom and pallor from her brow,
As, starting up and stretching out her arms,
She spoke *his* name, and then sank slowly down,
Still looking outward with the same rapt gaze,
Till Death and Evening shut the west from view!

The long years went; yet 'gainst the sky's blue edge
Still beat the waters with unceasing roar,
Like baffled prisoners 'gainst their dungeon-wall,
But, inward rolling, brought no tidings back;
And when full half a century had pass'd,
Some heirs of this forgotten venture, roused
By slight memorial of unknown fates,
Charged vessels northward-bound to solve their doom.
And so, one summer morn, a wandering bark
Through cracking icebergs' shadows safely steer'd,
And moor'd beside an island's barren shore;
In spite of fear, guided by snow-patch'd rock

Whereon two whiten'd skeletons were perch'd,
Towards eager search for relics, and here found,
Mid ruin'd beams, a mildew'd book, that told,
Half log, half journal, all the story sad
Of that old vessel and her long-lost crew;
Written by one who, as they gather'd there,
Was he that died the last on that lone spot.
In the world's history 'twas a little page;
But, as all human hearts know human pain,
Perchance to read what other lives endure
May give some fainting soul the patience meet
To share the common lot, and look to God!
And thus, as 'twere in that dead sailor's words,
I paint the scenes that happen'd long ago,
How other men have suffer'd ere they died.

We sail'd to seek new fortunes in new lands,
Won by our captain's promise of rich mines;
And 'mong our motley crew but two were free
From labor and delusive dreams of wealth.
The chaplain one, a man so slight of frame,
So pure in word and deed, we well might deem
That his unceasing prayer, his constant thought
Of higher things, had purged his life and flesh
Of all of passion, till his body seem'd
To be the willing slave of soul sublime.
We were not tender! we,—a boisterous set
Of untamed natures. Some had never known,
Or would not brook, restraint upon their sin;
And few had ever thought of aught beyond

The present, and but named their God in oaths!
Yet, when he came anear, the worst would hush
Their ribaldry, though never once he marr'd,
By useless preaching, laugh or harmless jest;
And when he left, there was a yearning sense
Of something softer in our inmost hearts,
That made us talk, e'en mid our reckless selves,
Of homes and mothers, wives and little babes;
For there is that in human creatures still,
Howe'er obscured by evil, that will bow
To aught superior, be it strength of limb
Or mind, and thrills when weakness seems to claim
Protection from its self-acknowledged power.
We bent before the goodness we believed,
And, as we all were hardy, strong, and large,
We had for him a feeling such as men
Who are not brutes for helpless women hold.

The other came on board with springing step
And lifted head, a sneer upon his lips,
And searching, sparkling eyes that never smiled.
We could not guess what country gave him birth,
So well he spoke the languages of all,
Knew every land and wave and name of stars,
Nor what the motive cast his lot with ours;
But we, the English of our motley crew,
Swore that his birthplace must have been the sea,
And all men foreign, since he show'd no love
For human thing, but knew each mast and spar,
And all the rules of sailing, as his home
Had only been upon a vessel's deck,

And that he restless roved to 'scape remorse!
He never gave his hand; and one who read
Arabian tales did notice at the mess
He touch'd no salt,—as if he would not share
The pledge of friendship with a living soul.
He seem'd to have strange sense of what was hid
And worst in all, and with his mocking speech
Would fright us with such reading of our thoughts
That something kin to fear compell'd his scorn.
And only once a quiver of surprise
Betoken'd passion 'neath the practised mask,
At sudden meeting of the chaplain's gaze.
I stood near by, and saw him grasp the arm
That shrank as from the touch of searing flame,
And, with a changed and eager voice, demand,
"Where is she, priest?—wedded, or mad, or dead?"
Slowly the white lips answer'd, "She has gone
To heaven!" and the livid, questioning face
Turn'd seaward from a look of pitying pain.
But quick the old tone came:—"You loved her once,
Or thought you did; but I, who had her thoughts
So long in life, am curious to know
Who kept them at her death: you held, 'tis true,
Advantage of your garb and circumstance,
Two potent spells to sway a woman's mind,
And I—Pshaw! how, when, died the girl? Canst tell?"
I saw the flushing of the thin, worn brow,
I saw the flashing of the soft, sweet eye,
I saw the clenching of the hand, and heard
The hard-drawn sigh that mark'd the end of strife,

Wherein true holiness self's instinct slew!
An instant's work,—yet, as for Christ's sole sake
I saw Christ's servant conquer nature thus,
I never once have ta'en Christ's name in vain!
Nor e'er forgot the thrilling voice that spoke:—
"I buried her, her baby on her breast;
I gave the new-born child its name,—your name,—
And closed their eyes together; she bless'd *you*
With her last, weak breath, dying forgave you,
And never thought of me, who watch'd her through
The gate of death, regardless of all sneers!"
Oh, what a groan tore from the callous heart,
As, like a wounded tiger in a cage,
He paced a moment's space the narrow deck,
Then, pausing full before the troubled face
That watch'd his own, hiss'd out his fiery words!
"Forget, or think of her—dost hear?—as *mine*,
Here and hereafter mine, who hates you still,
Though now I know desertion, doubt, and death
Ne'er gave you what you craved,—one dream of hers!"
And then he went—and, ere an hour had pass'd,
Was taunting a scarr'd Dane in his own tongue.
The while the other, leaning o'er the sea,
Did only seem to count the curling waves—
I knew he pray'd to God, as One before
Pray'd from the cross for those that nail'd Him there!

We sail'd and sail'd. Days grew to weary weeks.
The glittering stars were brighter; floating near,

The sparkling bergs oft cross'd our timid track,
Until one morn we woke to see our ship
Wedged in by icy walls, that crack'd and heaved,
And wore fantastic shapes that changed each hour,
But show'd no crystal door, with rainbows arch'd,
Whence we might 'scape into the open sea.
The constant fear, the eager, watching hope,
To sullen murmuring turn'd, as lack of work
Sent each man's musings towards his distant home,—
Till mutter'd threats grew loud, and oaths were sworn
That when the way was clear our course should be
No forward move, but back the path we came!
And here our captain died,—stung to his death
By cold accusing looks, and his own doubts;
For he did love all glory, but his thought
Leap'd ever to the end, nor counted means,
And where they slower proved than his desire,
Lost heart, nor fought 'gainst circumstance; and now
He fretted at the strait his dreams had brought,
And in his eyes there sadly gleam'd at times
Prophetic pity, till a quick remorse
Fed on the life we still were loath to lose.
We wrapp'd him in our flag, and let him down
In the green waters, where the shadows dark
Of those white mountains rested on his heart
As heavy as their presence on our own;
And in the drifting of those mighty isles
One may have paused above th' unconscious dust,
While from the diamond depths its awful voice

Proclaim'd to swelling winds, which dash'd the foam
Against its gothic carvings, that below
Was something far more fearful than itself,
Even great, silent Death! The little child
I saw him kiss at parting never knew
How grand a monument her father had!

Perchance that solemn something in the sea
Appall'd those frozen hearts, and stirr'd to flight;
For soon we toss'd upon the waves that heaved
Responsive to their passing Polar guests.
And scarce their snowy peaks escaped our view,
When 'neath the deck misrule and riot reign'd,
And cursing ruffians swore to turn the ship;
And all that strove the mutiny to quell
Were bound and silenced. As easy tame
A troop of hungry panthers round their prey!
We surged and roar'd a moment in mad glee,
And then, mid frantic shouts, it struck our sense
That still the ship moved on; and, as we deemed,
Command was conquer'd, all our weapons dropp'd
As up we press'd to gain our certain end!
Yelling with triumph, rush'd the foremost crowd
To seize the wheel—when, lo! undaunted, cool,
The stranger stood beside the helm, and eyed
Our sheer surprise, our sudden pause, with looks
Glittering and calm, the while one steady hand
Outheld a pistol, and his belt was stuck
Full of strange knives, some jewell'd to the blade.
We stood an instant, fallen back, and stunn'd,
Subdued by that keen glance that seem'd to chill

Each man's hot blood. Then one deep howl broke out;
We made one bound to tear him limb from limb,—
When o'er our raging tones his words rang clear:—
"Back, back, ye hounds! he dies the first who stirs!
I hold a dozen of such lives as yours,
And take them with me if I go myself!
Ye're ripe for Lucifer, ye snarling curs!"
What was there in the single figure there,
That seem'd to grow a giant in our sight,
Standing erect against the cloudless sky,—
What was there in that sneering, cutting voice,
Or in that fiery glance from which we shrank,—
To cow us down like dogs before this man?
Save that he show'd more reckless than ourselves!
Yet scarce we knew our master, ere he touch'd
The idle wheel, and quick we forward leap'd,
Then quail'd like cowards from that eye and death!
And, as we throng'd together in one mass,
His words fell in our midst again like shot!
"Look back, ye fools: behind, the icebergs lie,
Before, the open sea: there, certain wreck,
And here, a chance for life! Choose hell or earth!"
Our startled thoughts took in th' unstudied truth,
And, while we stood uncertain how to turn,
Abash'd, controll'd, a tender voice stole o'er
Our hope's despair, "Dear comrades, let us pray!"
And there, upon the deck so nearly stain'd
With crime and blood, our chaplain knelt alone.

Some bow'd their heads; some turn'd with mutter'd
 oaths;
The stranger wore a scoff upon his lip,
And with a dagger play'd, the while there rose
A mighty cry to God, that must have pierced
Through all the angels' songs and reach'd His
 throne!
I do believe that holy soul itself
Went up to His own footstool, and beheld
The glory of the highest heaven, so full
Of love, of radiance, the pale face shone,
Pleading for such as us, "his brethren,"—*his!*
And as with earnestness his voice grew low,
Guilt seem'd to move us far from him and Christ,
Till Christ's own words o'erflooded harden'd minds,
And rough men wept in uttering soft "Amens."
And, as his accents died upon the air,
Each man went slowly to his olden post.

And now we lived mid dangers. Day and night
The icebergs pass'd us, and the sea was full
Of floating hills, and gathering, broken ice;
And, worst of all, at last we sprung a leak,
And saw before us only wreck and death;
When, thrilling through our sullen mien, one morn
A single word fired every hopeless breast,
And brought upon the deck a motley group
Of eager faces, as the voice aloft
Sang out, once more, "Land straight ahead!" and
 then
One hearty cheer rang through the frozen air!

Land! any land! a firm, unshaken shore
A haven! life! Some trembled as they watch'd
Brown, barren rocks loom o'er the dashing waves,
Crested with snow, or shooting out great spurs
'Twixt silvery glaciers, while here and there
A mighty fracture made a shadow'd bay.
And so at last we came to land again!
Not a fair country! not a tree or shrub
To wave a welcome e'en with leafless boughs!
Only wide fields all white, white cliffs, white coasts,
Cold, traceless, desolate, and still, as though
A moment's magic changed the world to stone!
We call'd it "Marble Isle," because it spread
Beneath its gray and overhanging sky
Like to a sculptured dream. Alas! alas!
The name half-sportive fancy gave it then
Proved stern reality to after-hopes!

Our crippled bark could never sail again;
The shore was one bleak desert, and the chance
Of rescue fainter than we dared to feel;
And so we took the timbers for a hut,
With sea-weed thatch'd, and remnants of our sails;
A sort of wooden tent built round the mast,
That in the centre stood, and bore on high
Our English flag,—the warmest-tinted thing
That ever stirr'd amid that dreary waste!
And here, throughout the long and weary months,
We waiting sat around our drift-wood fire,
Or from the highest rock, with lingering hope,
Watch'd for a ship across the lonely sea.

It never came, and yet, with cheerful words,
As, daily, turning inland towards the night,
Each stifled down the sighs he would not breathe,
Lest he should rob his comrade of the trust
'Twere worse than death to lose, and kept us brave,
We lighten'd tedious evenings with old tales,
The stories of our lives, with every thought
And memory that could shorten lagging time.
Only the chaplain's eyes kept pure our talk,
Where each man made a confidant of all.
I think while he was with us that we felt
The sense of God's own presence; for he lived
So near to Him that all his words and deeds
Like inspiration seem'd; and when he told
The glories of the City of the King,
And pray'd with tearful voice to meet us there,
We listen'd with touch'd hearts, and strove to be
To one another more like him and Christ.
We loved him; for he kept alive the sparks
Of truth and tenderness, of something good
Within the worst, and made the hardest feel
Our grovelling natures could ascend to heaven.
And when we saw him fading day by day,
Worn by our hardships, though unmurmuring still,
And never thinking of himself, we grew
More careful o'er him, as we dimly knew
Our link with God would break if he should die.
His lip would quiver, and his pale cheek glow,
As some rough act of kindness or respect
Would prove us men that watch'd upon his face

The spirit's light reflected from the Throne;
And we were thank'd in knowing that he saw
Our better selves expanding 'neath the touch,
E'en mid that solitude, of grateful love.'

Only the stranger, living in our midst,
And yet apart, scarce noticed this pure soul
Or heard its teachings. He had shown at first
Such skill, such varied knowledge of all arts
Which help'd our comfort, fix'd our awed surprise,
That he had won a sort of right to mar
With wayward moods the peace was still in ours.
For he would break at times his silent mien,
That never else was shaken, with some tale
Or legend of far lands that chain'd our sense,—
Of ghosts and genii, robbers and their deeds,
And all dread things, save mention of himself!
But most he liked to paint earth's wildest scenes
And worst experience; for he would tell
Of virgin forests full of savage lairs;
Of stiffen'd ships and sailors round the Poles;
Or dreary deserts that had once been seas,
Where phantom vessels sail'd at midnight o'er,
And ghastly shapes environ'd every step,
While voices drew the weary traveller on
To deeper solitudes, to die with thirst
And mix his bones with those that strew'd the waste
Of old sea-monsters and forgotten men;
Or left him, else, beneath some mighty rock
That bore the likeness of a human face

And jabber'd at him with sepulchral tones,
Till fascinated terror reft his wits;
Or he would speak of horrid murders done
By pirate dirks in secret sea-shore caves,
That victim spirits might their treasures guard;
And count us o'er the ingots and the gems,
Till avarice forgot the blood and guilt,
And clutch'd an eager hand on fancied gain!
With air so suited to each startling tale
As thrill'd us into statues of mute fear;
And when he saw us, stalwart men, controll'd
By spells of his weird power, a scornful laugh
Shock'd shuddering consciousness into our frames;
And as that sharp, triumphant peal aroused
Our words still whisper'd with a sense of awe,
Quickly he'd pass amid the shrinking throng
To distant corner and to muttering sleep,
Or, dashing out into the frozen night,
Be follow'd by long sighs of glad relief,
Or looks of fearful hate as might be cast
By tempted souls on Satan's demon-form

One day, when, wearied of some hollow sport,
We lay in groups, and through our sadness surged
The ocean's sound, or human voice of seals,
That ever roused new wonder or remorse,
When, dying from our shots, their eyes look'd up
Reproachful as a woman's we had wrong'd;
And, while we mused, one bounded in our midst
To show a prize,—the blacksmith of our crew,
Strong-limbed, with voice harsh as his anvil-strokes,

He held as tenderly in his hard hand,
As might a child, a single little flower;
Telling, in soften'd, almost reverent, tones,
How he had found it on the bleak hill-side,
Just peeping at the sky amid the snow,
Blue as the far spring violets we knew;
And how the sight had almost made him weep,
That had not wept since his one sister died,
And he, a boy, pluck'd daisies on her grave!
And so he could not keep the daily watch,
Sure that he might not see a ship for tears,
But gather'd up this precious waif to stir
Our heavy hearts as it had touch'd his own.
And while he talk'd, we throng'd with eager looks
Round that frail blossom, that recall'd to each
His dearest thing on earth, and days gone by!
Its faint, sweet perfume seem'd the breath of home!
We saw no more the desolate, cold isle,
But trod with buoyant steps our native fields,—
We felt the sun shine on our own green land,—
No more were exiles, left to die afar,
But youth that wander'd in the shady lanes,
Listening soft sighs, or watching changing cheeks.
Rough as we were, upon our yearning mood
The gentle beauty of those fragile leaves
Came like the Switzer's song in foreign lands
To children of the Alps, and shook our souls
Till memory's rapture was akin to pain!—
At last, by general instinct, we all bore,
With words subdued, our priceless gift to him
Who soon would see the flowers bloom in heaven.

When first we laid it in his hand, it seem'd
He ne'er could fill his spirit with its grace,
But gazed and gazed till swell'd his forehead's
veins,
As glistening drops fell slowly on its stalk;
And then his broken words told naught in life
Had moved him like that plant amid the waste.

We placed it near the hearth-stone where we sat,
That all might see it; and it seem'd to lean
Towards our tones, as, lonely from its birth,
It found a comfort there. 'Twas like a babe
Laid in our midst, so soft it made our hearts;
We gently spoke, with awkward courtesy moved,
And eyes whose looks caress'd it oft were moist.
At length we ceased to talk; each man's own
thought,
Born of sweet fragrance, had become a dream;
When through our silence, from the outer night
That crept across the hills, the stranger stepp'd.
We stirr'd to let him seek the needed warmth,
And, as he stoop'd to see our treasure, watch'd
With curious gaze the fitful shadows limn'd
Upon his face before the leaping blaze.
It moved his nature's hidden depths, and shook
His guarded mien; 'twas as an angel's touch
Unseal'd a frozen fount; as he forgot
Our presence and the present, lived again
In other scenes akin to that pure thing!
Then, lifting up his head, he caught each glance,
And, as an angry flush betray'd self-scorn,

Spurn'd with his foot the flower into flames!
An instant we were all aghast; and then,
Cursing, we upright sprung, and, ere he turn'd,
A dozen axes gleam'd amid the glare!
He saw them raised, yet shrank not, leaning calm
With folded arms against the mast, and smiled
In sheer disdain of death, with that same look
Within his eyes that ruled us on the ship;
For once, he wore no weapons in his belt;
And yet we paused before this fearless man
That stood at bay, defying us and fate!
We would have spared him then, in very shame
Of numbers, and for his bravery's sake,
Save that he roused our fury with his taunts:
He joy'd that murder's sin should swell our woes;
And, as he pointed to the burning logs,
And call'd us girlish snivellers o'er a weed,
We rush'd again to drown his sneer in blood,—
When through the strife the chaplain urged his way,
And threw himself before the haughty breast,
That heaved in silence as the startling words
From quivering lips rang o'er our wrathful tones:—
"His life through mine! if ye must kill, slay me!"
Our blades dropp'd slowly; reverence conquer'd rage;
While o'er the stranger came a wondrous change.
His proud form trembled; something like a tear
Flash'd down his cheek; a cry, half groan, half sob,
Unstifled rose. as, bending on one knee,
He press'd a kiss upon the shadowy hand,

Then swiftly fled into the cold and dark!
And o'er the priest's worn brow there sudden broke
Seraphic glory, such as might have shone
On Moses' face when he had talk'd with God!
We gather'd round him with our clamorous tongues,
And one, the smith, sore from his blossom's loss,
Ask'd why he robb'd our vengeance of its due,
And what to him was such a worthless life,
That mid our anger he should risk his own.
The glow of rapture faded with a sigh:
"He was my enemy!" he humbly said.

The night waned slowly. Few had cared to sleep;
The rest sat silent, staring at the fire.
Outside 'twas bitter cold; a snow had fall'n
And spread the white earth with a thicker veil;
And round our hut the wind shriek'd shrill and fierce,
Or moan'd and wail'd, as though it shared our fate
And could not 'scape beyond these rock-bound shores!
And more than once the chaplain rose and look'd
Into the darkness with sad, anxious eyes,
Whose trouble beat against our sullen wills;
For hours pass'd, nor brought the absent back.
At length his heart could bear suspense no more,
And, standing in our midst, he made appeal,
For mercy's sake and his, that we would seek,
While yet was time, our comrade, who perhaps
Was lost, or struggling in some drift for life!
That little flower had done its mission well,

In softening men as rough and hard as we;
And all our tender thoughts of home conspired
To make us listen to that pleading voice.
We hated him that we were ask'd to save,
But, then, we loved the other, and, besides,
Our passion over, some had just been glad
We had not slain the man that steer'd our ship
Through awful dangers even to this port!
And his one burst of nature wiped away
The thousand insults of his callous past.
And so we went,—at first with lagging steps
And minds reluctant, that were 'shamed to stay,
Or fear'd their own reproach if one should die
While we sat housed and warm. But soon the hunt
Stirr'd eager blood, and towards its end we toil'd
Through changing dangers as for dearest friend!—
We search'd and shouted; but the hills alone
Made answer with their echoes, till there broke
A tinge of dawn across the eastern heights;
And as we threw aside our torches dim
That cast their flickering glare upon the snow,
The priest had seized the nearest idle spade,
To delve amid a heap shaped like a grave;
We aided him in silence, help'd him draw
A stiffen'd form from 'neath its stainless pall,
And as we gazed upon the still, white brow,
We all forgot the worst in him, and saw
Only the calm and sadness that was left
By death's last touch upon the scornful face!
And in his hand, tight clasp'd upon his heart,

A long, soft lock of woman's golden hair!—
That shook us! there scarce was one but thought
Of some fair head he ne'er would see again;
As, bending o'er it, frost and wind unfelt,
Tears started unawares, and, falling, froze
Amid our shaggy beards; while some who held
No pure remembrances, in wonder stared
To see such jewel shine on such a breast!
And we forgave the dead because he too
Had loved and lost! And they were gentle hands
That laid him in the earth, and reverent brows
That bow'd as rose upon the rising day
The priest's grand, earnest prayer that God would give
The wanderer perfect rest; the while we felt,
With gathering sense of gloom, that this first link
Thus sever'd in our brotherhood of pain
Foretold the doom of all: we too would sleep
In tombs of ice, while the world's life went on!

The blossom first, and then the silken tress
That we had buried on that pulseless heart,
Had stirr'd the deepest feelings of our souls,
And made our yearnings grow till I have seen
Our strongest steal away to weep alone.
And, spite of all our efforts to endure
With manly patience for each other's sake,
There slowly fell a sort of still despair
Upon our lives, and show'd in all our ways,
Until we could not bear at last to look
Into each other's eyes, lest we should read

All that we felt was written in our own!
Then other troubles came; starvation's dread
Help'd kill our hope; and then our pastor died.
I mark'd him when his startled sight first saw
That lovely hair, and o'er the pallid face
A flood of memories swept that broke at last
His strain'd control in one unstifled sigh;
And while we dug the grave, he trembling stroked
With timid fingers its soft, wavy length.
And since that hour his life had faded fast,
Like one that sees a spirit, and then pines
Until he joins it at the gate of death!—
We tended him as mothers might a child
Left orphan'd on their care, or as of old
The patriarchs had served an angel guest,—
Gave him our best, and grieved that 'twas so poor;
And at the last thank'd God our store held out
Till he was gone and never knew the worst!
The while he pray'd with us, clasp'd each man's hand
And spoke a word to him none e'er forgot;
And if such souls as ours shall ever walk
Amid the shining ones where he will be,
And doubt to know him in his glory's change,
We shall but speak that word to see his face
Glow tender with its human smile again;
And if, perchance, he take our hand once more
Before the host of God, why, we shall stand
Prouder in heaven than if crown'd on earth!
And near the end he call'd from out our midst
A stubborn, silent nature, and laid down

His head upon the breast, just touching first
With his white lips the coarse and trembling mouth;
And as the broad chest swell'd beneath his brow,
Death's shadow fell across his waiting soul,
Darkening our day, but making his all light.

And afterwards we died so fast—O God,
How couldst Thou dwell amid the bliss of heaven,
Watching our wretchedness, and never send
A single ship across those barren seas!
The dull suns rose and set in low, gray skies;
The mocking waters beat on frozen shores;
The white hills lean'd against the drooping clouds
In their eternal stillness,—while we died!
Surely we were not worse than other men
Who sleep among their kindred, that no place
Save this was found for us to die upon!
Earth is so wide, and full of lovely spots,
Green, clustering woods, and meadows gold with grain,
And sunny dells with cots half hid in vines,
And rippling streams with flowers on their banks:
Yet far from these our lot on this lone isle!
For all our shot gave out, and e'en the seals
Forsook at last these desolate, bleak coasts!
And then we died, starved of all food and hope!—
The blacksmith first, we found him cold and stiff
Upon the chaplain's grave, where he had gone
To cut the name upon the stone we rear'd
Rough-hewn into a cross,—his task just done!
Then he who held our saint within his arms

And caught his last pure breath: he scarcely spoke
Since we had lifted that pale, precious form
From 'neath his dropping tears, until he crept
Close to the dead man's robes, that still were hung
Against our smoke-stain'd wall, and, reaching up,
Touch'd with weak hand the garment's hem, and pray'd,
Gasping and faint, that he might meet again
God's blessed angel that had been on earth!
And one died cursing, hurling bitter oaths
Against the Maker who could doom His work
To cruel torture, deaf to groans and cries;
Or swore there was no God but devilish Fate,
That made a sport of human pain and woe,
And naught beyond the welcome chill of Death!
And two went mad, and cast them raving down
From jutting cliffs into the ice-strewn waves
That toss'd their mangled bodies back to land!
And some sat patient, waiting for their hour,
Haggard and quiet, brave from sheer despair,
With tighten'd belts, and bony hands firm link'd
In some old comrade's they had known at home!
And they that kept their strength a while did naught
But toil at graves till ready for their own!
And there were wolfish looks in sunken eyes,
That roused an unnamed fear, when we ourselves,
Frantic with want, the savage instinct felt;
For hunger made us murderers in our thought,
And each man hid a weapon, lest his life
Should aid the rest to live; and so we walk'd

Apart in gloom, and ceased to count the deaths.
It was a dreadful thing to wake at morn
From fitful slumber full of horrid dreams,
To find new dead, and wonder 'twas not us,—
To lift with feeble arms those rigid frames
And bury them from sight in tombs of snow
That stood like marble sepulchres in rows,—
To live amid the dying, gaunt as they,
And keep our senses mid such awful sights,
And something still of faith, by saying o'er
To our own souls some words our pastor spoke,
Or simple teachings from our mothers' lips!

At last we were but two; with wasted limbs
We bore a third one to his place of rest,
And, as we stood beside the new-made grave,
We weary look'd into each other's face;
No need for speech,—the sad sea-sound said all;
We dropp'd our spades, clasp'd hands across the mound,
And turn'd away together towards the rock
Where we were wont to keep our fruitless watch;
Not that we hoped a ship would come to us
That never cheer'd the rest; but habit led
Our failing footsteps to our old look-out,
And we were not so lonely as when day,
Dying with dull, red flush upon the waves,
Sent us again to our forsaken hut;
And when the morning came, we sought once more
Our seat upon the crag, to find escape
From solemn company of ghosts and graves;

And as we silent sat there, waiting death,
My comrade sudden dropp'd his fainting head
Down on my breast. I call'd his name, I look'd
With thrills of terror on his pallid lips,
Had never stirr'd my blood when others died;
For, though I knew our hours were number'd, still
Such keen fear seized me to be left alone,
That great drops bathed my brow, the while I pray'd
Aloud in my strong anguish,—and he woke;
And, gazing from my bosom o'er the deep,
Said, in a voice that had a dying tone,
"One keeps a tryst with me whom I thought false;
I saw her even now, on rock like this,
She and an old gray sailor who had wound
His arm about her as yours thus holds me;
She saw me here, and stretch'd her dear hands out.
Think of it, friend, that all this watery waste
Kept not our souls apart! We will meet now.
Sweet heart, she waited long!—to-night my eyes
Will look in hers as in the olden time!—
Thanks—you were always kind,—shake hands once more:
God bless you, Jack—how dark it is!—good-bye!"

I would not think him dead; I held him close,
Rubbing his hands, and saying to myself,
"'Tis but another swoon; he soon will wake!"
But I, alas! had seen too many die
To keep delusion long. And so at last
I lean'd him gently up against the rock,

Still looking towards our England and his love!
I could not bury him: I had no strength.
I could not weep: I e'en was starved of tears.
I could not stay there, and go slowly mad.
So I have come with faltering steps once more
To this sad shed, to sit beside the mast,
And underneath our tatter'd, faded flag!
Its colors were so bright when first unfurl'd!
Ah! who would then have deem'd 'twould wave alone,
That fair, frail thing, o'er all our perish'd hopes!
'Tis like a friend, and I can pity feel
That it must still float on when I am gone!—
My God, how lonely 'tis here! I have heard
That men have lived thus upon desert isles;
But then they dwelt not in the midst of graves!—
I think I know now how the last man felt
In the great Flood, watching the waters rise!
Did God seem near him as He does to me!—
Outside, the grand hills lift their heads to heaven;
And years will roll, still the same skies will touch
Those snow-crown'd crests, when we will be but dust!
Ah no! Ye hills, I shall outlive ye all!—
How white my native cliffs shone in the sun
That day we sail'd! what green fields lay behind!—
I wonder if they think of me sometimes
In that dear English farm-house far away!
I wonder if my mother's sitting yet
Beside the hearth, and dropping, as she knits,
A tear of memory on the home-spun yarn!

And if she keeps the shells upon her shelf
I brought on my first voyage! How proud she was
E'en of my sailor walk! Thank God, a tear!
And, oh! what pain! my dizzy brain reels round!—
I see strange visions: do the dead come back!—
Nay, 'tis but weakness! I cannot die here!—
I must go back to our look-out, and sit
Beside my comrade, with my face towards home!—
Perhaps the tardy ship may come too late,
And those aboard may take our exiled bones,
For sweet compassion's sake, to our own shores!—
Ah! hunger's pangs are sharp! I faint again!—
One more last look, and then I must be gone,
Or I shall fail to drag me up the steep.
There are the ashes of our last, bright fire,
There the rough seats we sat on; 'gainst the wall
Still hangs the chaplain's robe; and here and there
A worn, stain'd jacket, as if just thrown off.
Farewell, poor objects that have e'en grown dear!
Farewell, old stunted pen that wrote this log,—
The saddest, sure, was ever kept by man!
Farewell, my country's flag! Life, life, farewell!

THE END.